ROGUE HEARTS

ALYSE ZAFTIG

CONTENTS

CHAPTER 1

VICTORIA

"ALL RISE for the Honorable Judge William Hughes."

Victoria Bellamy stood at the command of the bailiff, and the judge came in with his long, black robe and sat in the burgundy leather chair behind the podium. His face was stern and determined. Despite his forbidding appearance, Victoria was happy Hughes was the judge she got. He was a stern overseer, and criminals never got off easy with him ruling the courtroom.

Her trial would go well as long as she stayed alert. She'd even worn her lucky royal navy suit, the one that she used to boost her confidence on the first day of her court cases.

"You may be seated," the bailiff said.

Judge Hughes gave instructions to the jury about the laws and rules that apply to this case and then turned to look at her and the defense.

"We will now hear Prosecuting Attorney Victoria Bellamy present the case of the People versus Roman Vasin," the judge said.

As Victoria stood and made her way to the floor before speaking, she noticed that the defense attorney with the curly blond hair was staring at her. She had done her research on Andrei Rusak before coming into the courtroom. She knew he was representing his family law firm, which had a history of defending powerful men. Going over his information helped her prepare for the trial. What she wasn't expecting was the way he followed her every move with his eyes or the fact that he'd be better looking than the photos she found on him. She felt butterflies in her stomach when she looked at him, but her attraction to him was wildly inappropriate on so many levels. She pushed all of that to the back of her mind as she mentally prepped for her opening statement.

She made eye contact to reinforce her don't-fuck-with-me lucky suit and matching shoes. In the past, defense attorneys underestimated her, especially the men. She'd built her reputation brick by brick. She wanted it to be clear that she knew how to do her job and do it well. It all started with the clothes followed by a heap of confidence... not just the bravado new lawyers had to make themselves seem smart. True confidence in the courtroom came from dealing with the strong wins and the shitty failures, which she used with every move she made in front of the courtroom.

"Your Honor, ladies and gentleman of the jury," Victoria started, "today the people are charging Roman Vasin with willful and deliberate first degree murder of Samuel Winter." Victoria took her time to walk the length of the jury section. When she moved in front the jury and made eye contact with every one of them, she glimpse out of the side of her eye and noticed Rusak was still staring at her.

"The people will prove beyond a reasonable doubt that Roman Vasin killed Samuel Winter with malice by calling our witnesses." She listed her key witness, Mr. Ollie Jefferson, who allegedly saw Mr.

Vasin throwing the duffle bag containing the body into the Hudson River. He was the one who was going to help her win. Detectives from the New York Police Department Diving team, who retrieved the duffel bag containing the body from the Hudson River, the coroner who did the autopsy, and an expert from ballistics, who identified the type of weapon and the bullets used in the shooting, rounded out her witness team. "We will also be using the film from the security cameras in and around the jewelry store to help prove our case."

She couldn't stop a small smile from making an appearance when she sat down, so she looked at her court files to hide it. This moment was why she enjoyed her job. It wasn't for the noble reasons of putting bad guys away or seeing justice done. Those were great, but it was the thrill of knowing that she did her job well. That got her through some of the craziness that came from being a prosecutor.

When Victoria sat down, she felt confident in her opening statement. She had this case locked down. There was no way any jury would find Vasin innocent after all the evidence she'd gathered.

Even as she sat down, she still felt the defense attorney's eyes on her, and they were completely glued to her. Instead of letting it get to her, she finally turned to him and stared right back at him, ice glittering in her eyes. She was expecting an answering challenge in his eyes, but she found something less threatening. He smiled warmly back at her before the judge called him up. She was taken aback, blinking a little bit. When he smiled at her, it felt like the sun had just come out from behind the clouds.

When the defense attorney stood up, she realized how tall and handsome he really was. A lean figure rested underneath his expensive, gray, suit that melded to his solid body like fine butter with deliciously broad shoulders filling out the top of him as if he wasn't a stranger to occasional weightlifting. He had sexy cheekbones and strong features that made him handsome without being drop-dead gorgeous or a delicate pretty boy.

There was something about him that made it hard for her to take her eyes off him.

"Your Honor," he said, "ladies and gentlemen of the jury, I am Andrei Rusak, the defense attorney for Mr. Vasin, and this is my defense team: Attorneys Linda Lamb and Roslyn Thompson." He glanced her way. "Unlike the prosecution, I'm here to prove my client is innocent. The evidence is circumstantial and doesn't place my client anywhere near the scene of the crime."

Victoria held back a scoff, and she continued listening as he noted witnesses for his defense.

As soon as the he completed his statement, Vasin jumped out of his seat, and screamed, "I didn't do it, Your Honor!"

The judge picked up the gavel and hammered it down a couple of times. "Order in the court, Mr. Vasin, you cannot yell in the courtroom. Mr. Rusak, I suggest you explain to your client that I expect a civilized trial from here on out."

"Of course, Your Honor," Rusak said as he pulled Vasin back down in his seat and whispered something in his ear. Vasin mumbling something back and seemed angry, his face still flushed. Not a minute later, he jumped up again and yelled out, "I didn't kill anyone, Your Honor!"

"Keep him quiet," said the judge, "or I will hold him in contempt!"

"It won't happen again, Your Honor." This time it was Rusak's turn to get angry as he whispered into Mr. Vasin's ear and pulled the man back down with a hand clamped to the back of Vasin's neck.

Victoria figured he was explaining to his client that contempt meant jail time along with a possible fine for being disruptive. If it continued like this, the case would be easier than she thought and certainly an entertaining experience.

Vasin stayed silent and remained down this time. One reason why Victoria liked being a prosecutor was that the state was her client and not some spoiled man-child who had too much money and power for the span of his lifetime.

Victoria watched Rusak as he stood back up and moved around the courtroom floor to initiate his defense. He made sure that he faced the judge and the jury before finally settling his startlingly blue eyes back on her. She could feel her heart beating hard in her chest and her breathing deepening. Inappropriate. So inappropriate to feel this way.

The way he looked at her made it seem like he saw straight through to some deeper part of her that no one else could see. It was a stare that would make anyone want to look away from feeling so vulnerable, but Victoria made sure she kept his gaze.

She thought she saw a small, crooked smile on the side of his mouth before he turned to the others in the courtroom. What was that all about?

With each look, he was making her things she had long since pushed to the side so she could focus on her career. Her last relationship had been her longest and hadn't ended well. They didn't talk at all anymore. After the dust had settled, she had chosen to forget about her love life and focus on work, which had helped her get to where she was now. The way Rusak kept staring at her made her wonder if she had done the right thing.

She crossed her legs, pushing back the warmth that had stirred up there. She was in court. There was no place for the thoughts that were popping up in her head. Besides, the guy who strode back and forth in front of her was the defense, her opposition.

His blond hair fell forward, and he gently took his hand and brushed his hair back from his face. It was a simple gesture, but he made it appear tempting and almost seductive.

As he continued to speak, she noticed his lips. They were full and pouty lips that any woman would love kissing. She wondered what those lips would feel like kissing her neck. She could feel the edge of excitement creep up through her as she listened to his baritone voice.

She closed her legs as if anyone would be able to sense the wetness that had built up beneath her freshly-pressed skirt. Okay, it had been a while for her, and her body was painstakingly reminding her of that fact. She adjusted her blouse, feeling the room get warm.

This time when he turned and looked at her, he licked his lips. Oh, he knew exactly what he was doing. Maybe it was a tactic to throw her off, or maybe he was one of those men who thought all women should fall at his feet. She didn't know whether it was an intentional distraction or not, but it was working. She was better than this, and she wasn't going to let him mess with her, no matter how attractive he was. Her face and neck flushed, making the room feel like a sauna.

"What the hell is wrong with me?" she thought. "I have got to stop this daydreaming. Get it together, Victoria. It's game time." She silently blamed it on lack of sleep and tried to focus on his words rather than the voice forming them.

Andrei Rusak continued his opening defense. "The prosecution would have you believe that Mr. Roman Vasin is guilty for the crime of murder, but we will prove otherwise. The neurologist will testify of the nerve damage in my client's hands and spine, thus preventing him from shooting anyone or having the strength to pick up a body and throw it in the river. My witnesses will also testify that Mr. Vasin attended their wedding on the day in question and spent the night at the family estate for two days at a location that is six and a half hours away in Buffalo."

When the defense finished, the judge called over the bailiff. "Why is it so hot in here, Bailiff?"

It wasn't just her. The courtroom was more than a

little warm, and the air conditioner didn't feel like it was functioning at full capacity.

Victoria had already unbuttoned the top part of her shirt without revealing anything that would make her seem unprofessional. Still, a bead of sweat trickled down her temple.

A few people were even fanning themselves with papers, and the jury shifted uncomfortably in their seats.

"I'm sorry, Your Honor," the bailiff said. "Maintenance was supposed to come in and fix it yesterday."

"Well, we can't continue in here under these conditions. The jury will have heat stroke before we even get to the first witness." The judge dismissed the bailiff. "We will continue with a few breaks in between this session. If it becomes too much, we will adjourn for a future date. Now, the prosecution will call the first witness."

Victoria did her best to focus on the case rather than how hot she was getting. She tried to do as little movement as possible to keep from overheating.

"The footage from the security cameras will be shown and entered as exhibit number one," she said. "It shows Vasin—"

Rusak interrupted saying, "I object. The man in the security footage has not been identified as my client."

Judge Hughes said, "Sustained. Ms. Bellamy, you will rephrase your statement."

"I apologize, Your Honor. I will say it another way." She stared at Rusak. "You claim that you saw the alleged suspect" she started before turning back to her witness, "entering the jewelry shop, shooting the victim, stuffing him into a beige duffle bag, and then dragging him out back and placing him in the truck bed. Is that correct?"

"Yes," her witness said. "I saw it just like that. I saw him leaving the back alley behind Winters Jeweler driving a white truck."

"To be specific, you said a white Ford pickup. Is that right?

"Yes."

"He was later seen dumping a large, beige duffle

bag into the Hudson River. Later, a beige duffle bag was retrieved by the New York police department, bearing the body of Sam Winter, who was found shot twice in the torso."

Vasin jumped up and screamed out, "No! No! No! That's a lie. All lies."

The courtroom broke out in gasps and murmurs.

Judge Hughes banged his gavel repeatedly. "Order in the court. Order in the court! That's it. Bailiff, take Mr. Vasin into custody. He will be charged with contempt of court and pay a fine of no greater than $500. Maybe that will teach you to hold your tongue in my courtroom. This isn't a court drama, Mr. Vasin. Maybe Mr. Rusak and your defense team need to remind you of that before you reappear in front of me. Until then, Mr. Rusak, it may be in the best interest to have your client submitted for a mental evaluation since he has problems following simple directions?"

Mr. Rusak said, "Yes Your Honor."

Victoria bit her lip to keep from laughing. Her case was turning into a circus, and it hadn't even been

an hour in session yet. She couldn't wait to tell her
friends about this one.

CHAPTER 2

ANDREI

ANDREI RUSAK WAS BEGINNING to question his own sanity in addition to his client's. The man was beginning to be a pain in the ass, and it was Andrei's job to get the man off from a murder case. Maybe his best option was to plead insanity after his random outbursts.

The only silver lining was the sexy prosecutor, Victoria Bellamy. She had her own reputation for giving criminals what they deserved. He'd heard about her and done his own little prodding about her, but this was the first time he'd seen her in action, and he was impressed already.

He knew he should just keep to himself and focus on helping his client, but he couldn't take his eyes off her. The suit she had on hugged her curves in all the right places. He wondered if she would feel soft and delicious up against his body.

He could tell he was getting under her skin a little by staring, and he had to admit he enjoyed that a little too much. It wasn't his intention to mess with her or ruin her presentation. In fact, he did it for selfish reasons. Andrei wanted to see if she responded to his attentions, and he had confirmation of that.

The judge had taken an hour recess to get control back in the courtroom. Andrei used that time to knock some sense into his client.

The man and his family had been close friends with his father for years, and his father had made him take the case. Andrei wasn't a big fan of the Vasins. They were a little too privileged and snobby for them to really feel like his friends. To him, they were just more people his father knew that he had to represent. Sometimes he enjoyed defending people he knew were innocent. Other times they got to be a pain in his ass.

"What the hell is wrong with you?" he asked Roman.

"I can't just sit there while they try to call me a murderer." Roman paced back and forth in his tiny cell.

Andrei gripped the bars to keep from grabbing Roman and shaking some damn sense into him. "Actually, that's exactly what you're going to do. You're going to sit there and let me do my job. That means you don't speak unless you're up on that witness stand, unless you want to piss the judge off more than you already have. If that's your goal, you're finding yourself another lawyer, because I have no time for this bullshit."

Roman shook his head. "No, my father says you're the best person to handle my case, and I want the best."

"Then you'll listen to what I tell you and not act out like that again. Do you understand?"

Roman nodded.

"Good. We're in recess. When you get back out there, I want you quiet as a monk who has taken a vow of silence, or I'm leaving you here on your own. Your dad can find you someone else."

When Roman was allowed to enter the courtroom, Andre was pleased to see the man knew how to follow instructions. He sat quietly and didn't say a word. If he hadn't learned to shut up, the case would've turned into a nightmare for both of them. Although the jury made the decision, the judge could also make it harder for them. This judge was known for low tolerance for criminal activity and giving out harsh sentences. If Roman kept pushing it and was found guilty, he'd be at Judge Hughes' mercy.

"We will proceed with court," said Judge Hughes said after they all returned from the brief recess.

Judge Hughes said, "The defense will call their first witness."

Andrei stood and addressed the court. "I call Mrs. Rita Jackson to the stand."

As she approached the bailiff, he swore her in. "Please raise your right hand, and place your left hand on the Bible. Do you solemnly swear to tell the truth, the whole truth and nothing but the truth, so help you God?"

Mrs. Jackson said "I do" before taking a seat on the witness stand.

"You may be seated," the bailiff said.

Andrei straightened his suit. "Mrs. Jackson, will you tell the court where you were on May 14th?"

"I was getting married in Buffalo, New York."

"Could you name the person in this courtroom who was in attendance?"

"Roman Vasin was a guest at my wedding," she said.

There was a small uproar in the courtroom.

Judge Hughes slammed the gavel down "Order in the court!"

Andrei turned to the witness. "Could you please point to the defendant, so we have a clear view of who you mean?"

Mrs. Jackson pointed to his client. "It was Mr. Vasin, the man in the pinstripe suit."

Andrei kept his smile to a minimum and said. "No further questions, you may take your seat." He waited for her to step down. "I would like to call my next witness: Mr. Barry Jackson."

The bailiff approached the bench. "Mr. Barry Jackson, please raise your right hand and place your left hand on the Bible. Do you solemnly swear to tell the truth, the whole truth and nothing but the truth, so help you God?"

"I do," Mr. Jackson said.

"You may be seated."

Andrei waited for him to settle in. "Mr. Jackson, could you tell the court where you were on May 14th?"

Mr. Jackson replied, "I was getting married in Buffalo to my wife, as she stated earlier."

"Thank you for confirming that. Your wife stated that my client was a guest at your wedding. Can you confirm that?"

"Yes, I can. I have pictures taken by our photographer and multiple guests to prove it."

"Let the court note the pictures are evidence, which shows my client with the wedding party."

He presented the pictures to the judge. "In addition, a timestamp in on some of them to show the date they were taken."

"Objection, Your Honor," the prosecutor said. "We had no prior knowledge of such pictures."

"Approach the bench," Judge Hughes said, beckoning to him and the prosecutor. "Your client has already had two outbursts in my courtroom, and now you're presenting this without letting the prosecution examine the evidence? It should've been sent to them during discovery."

"We've only just received them, Your Honor," Andrei said. He left off that he had to use some untraditional methods to pull the bride and groom away from their extended honeymoon, but that was not important.

"If you have pictures of your client being in another place, then how do you explain the use of his gun and pick-up truck during the murder?" Judge Hughes asked.

"I'd like to see your client testify about that discrepancy," Prosecutor Bellamy said. "Unless he has a surprise twin we don't know about."

He smiled down at her, which made her shift. "Ms. Bellamy, Your Honor, I have a formal complaint reported by Mr. Vasin about a break in that occurred to his home just about the time of the murder, which was when his truck, gun and several other items were stolen from his home."

"I saw the papers." Bellamy said. "That seems pretty convenient."

Andrei handed the report papers to the judge, who read over them carefully.

Judge Hughes stated. "Since this means this catastrophe of a case can end sooner rather than later, I'll allow it, but your client must take the stand first."

Andrei nodded, "Yes, Your Honor." He could practically see the fumes coming from the prosecutor. This wasn't going her way at all, and he took a little bit of pride at being the one to throw her off her game. He liked a challenge, and he could sense the same from her. Neither of them liked to lose. That meant someone was going to leave that courtroom disappointed; it wasn't going to be him.

"Let the court enter these papers as exhibit number four," Judge Hughes said. "Mr. Vasin, approach the witness stand, and I'm warning you, one wrong action and I'll have you thrown back in lockup. Understood?"

"Yes, Your Honor," Roman said as he made his way to the stand.

The bailiff approached the bench, "Mr. Roman Vasin, please raise your right hand and place your left hand on the Bible. Do you solemnly swear to tell the truth, the whole truth and nothing but the truth, so help you God?"

"I do." He sat down and looked at Andrei uncomfortably.

"Mr. Vasin, how did your pick-up truck and gun manage to be involved in this murder?"

"I am not sure. All I know is that while I was away at the wedding, my house was broken into. At that time, those items along with my safe and stamp collection were stolen."

Judge Hughes sighed. "After looking over the certified documentation and hearing from the accused, I now call this case dismissed." He took his gavel and banged it once and said "Court adjourned."

CHAPTER 3

VICTORIA

VICTORIA HAD BEEN side-armed and hadn't even expected it. She was prepared to take this idiot all the way through a full trial.

She stood a little under five feet, but she never let anyone intimidate her for it. Her cocoa-brown skin wasn't common in the District Attorney's office either, but she wasn't there for anyone's entertainment. That's why they called her Pitbull Bellamy.

She made sure she worked out when she could, but she never starved herself. Besides, she loved her curves since they made her feel more confident. Her breasts sometimes felt a little too large for her small size, but she'd found a way to make sure they weren't too obvious to distract the men she encountered in a male-dominated profession. Extremely supportive sports bras were her closest friends. Over the past few years she dated occasionally, but nothing serious had ever come out of any of the dates, because she had buried herself into her work.

As she packed up, she could sense the defense's eyes still on her as he talked to her client. Of course the one guy she thought was handsome would be the one to ruin her case. She needed a drink with her friends after the long day she was having.

She left the courtroom and went straight to the bathroom to splash cold water on her face. She wouldn't be surprised if the heat made the judge speed the case up. New York heat was something else. With the close concrete buildings and asphalt in between them, it was a heat nightmare every summer.

But it wasn't just the heat that had her flustered. "Get it together, Victoria." She looked in the mirror, hoping to regain some sense of control. Yeah, she definitely needed a cold alcoholic drink and fast. She rushed out of the bathroom and ran smack into something hard, which knocked her on the floor.

"Ow!" She grabbed her ankle as a sharp pain raced through it. "Watch where you're going you—"

"I think you were coming out just as fast," a familiar voice said.

She looked up to see Andrei Rusak and those penetrating blue eyes staring at her as he knelt down to help her.

"Of course it's you," she muttered under her breath.

"I'm sorry," he said. "I didn't see you. Forgive me."

Great, she thought. He has to lay the sweetness on thick so I feel like the mean one. He's the kind prince charming. I'm the wicked witch.

"Here, let me help you up."

He didn't give her a chance to respond. Two strong arms lifted her up from the floor as if she weighed nothing at all, until she was standing up. It was so quick and efficient that she forgot the pain in her ankle.

Until she put her weight on it.

"Ow, ow. Damn it." She didn't care that people were looking at her as her voice echoed. She was in pain.

"Did I hurt you?" He assisted her to a bench in the hallway and began picking up her brief case, pocketbook and scattered folders. He had literally knocked the wind out of her.

"Are you alright?"

She was staring into space trying to catch her breath. Just because she could handle hardened criminals in the courtroom didn't mean she liked pain, and this was something that had her head spinning.

"I think I hurt my ankle," she said.

He slid her shoe off as if he'd done it many times before. "Yeah. It looks swollen. Stay here. I'll be back."

Where was she going to go? She couldn't even stand up. Just when she was trying to figure out where he went, he came back with a bag of ice, paper towels, and a bottle of water.

"Here," he said, handing her the bottle. "Drink this."

"Demanding aren't we?" she asked.

"After being in that inferno courtroom, I'm sure you're dehydrated. Drink up while I take care of your ankle." He didn't wait to see if she obeyed. Instead, he elevated her leg into his lap and placed the ice on her swollen ankle.

"Cold, cold." She gasped at the shock and tried to move away, but he held her in place.

"I know, but it'll keep the swelling down." He took the ice off and wrapped it with the paper towel. "Is that better?"

All she could do was nod.

"Good. The ice compress should keep it from swelling more until I can get you to the hospital."

"What?"

"I'm taking you to the ER to have it x-rayed. It might be broken."

"No. I'm perfectly fine—"

"Sit still," he commanded. He held her ankle gently and wouldn't take his eyes away from it.

Victoria lost track of how long he held it. She finally opened the water and took a sip. After feeling how refreshing it was, she took a few bigger gulps until she downed half of it.

When she was done, she saw him smiling up at her.

"See? Dehydration is a silent killer."

His fingers grazed her ankle and sent tiny sparks up her leg until they settled in her belly. She shifted under his touch.

"Now, prop your leg up here and keep the ice on it." He turned her around so her ankle stayed up on the bench. He placed her hand on the cold pack. "I'm going to the parking deck to get my car and bring it around to the side door. Then I will be back. Okay?" he said.

"Yes, that's fine." It wasn't ideal, but she wasn't sure what to do. What if her ankle was really broken? The last thing she wanted was an ambulance to come and make a scene about getting her. That bit of gossip would make it to her office before she even reached the hospital.

It only took a few moments for him to bring the car around. From the look of it, you'd think he took great pride in rescuing damsels in distress. He grabbed her stuff and lifted her off the bench.

"Hey! What are you doing?"

"I could let you hobble to my car, but it's faster if I carry you," he said.

She didn't know what to do. She didn't want to hurt herself before she got to the hospital, but if he carried her out of the courthouse, her colleagues would never let her hear the end of it. She just knew it.

Being close up against him had her flustered again, but it wasn't from the heat this time. She could feel the outline of his muscular chest pressing into her side. She'd been mistaken earlier. He probably weight-lifted and exercised on a regular basis the way he felt.

"North Eastern Medical is the closest hospital to

us," he said, pulling her out of her moment of body analysis. "Is that one alright?"

"Yes, that's fine, Mr. Rusak," she said.

He chuckled. "I think it's safe to go by our first names now. Call me Andrei."

"Andrei," she said, testing it out.

"Can I call you Victoria?"

She thought about it for a second. "Since you're literally carrying me, I guess it'll be fine."

"Why do I get the feeling you're a tough one to please?" he asked as he sat her in the front seat.

She took the seat belt from him and clicked it herself. "It comes with the job," she said. He didn't say anything else as he closed her door and went around to the driver's seat.

The hospital wasn't that far away, so they got there fairly quickly. He pulled up to the emergency room drop-off area. "We need a wheelchair please," he said to an emergency room attendant who came out. "I think she has a broken ankle."

The attendant rushed back in and came out with

the wheelchair. With both Andrei and the attendant there helping her out of the car, she felt like an invalid.

"I am going to park the car and come right in," Andrei said.

"You don't have to do that," she said.

"I know I don't have to. I want to."

She didn't know how to respond to that, so she let the attendant push her to the intake window. It was a miracle the emergency room wasn't busy. If there'd been some sort of shoot-out, she would've had to wait a while with an ankle that might or might not be broken. She wouldn't be at the top of the triage list. She was lucky that a possibly broken bone put her at the top of the list for now.

They took her information and carried her straight back for x-rays. The swelling had increased since she couldn't have the ice on it in the car, and she was having more pain now. The nurses gave her new ice packs, something for the pain, and a pill to help with the swelling.

She waited in the sterile room for the doctor to see

her. She hated hospitals, the way they looked and smelled, like death, urine, and cleaning supplies. Waiting alone in this empty room was starting to irk her. After what felt like forever, the doctor finally came in to discuss the results.

"Hello, Ms. Bellamy. I'm Dr. Smith,"

"Please tell me it's not broken. I have too much to do this week."

"Well, you're going to need to stay off it for a few days first. It's not broken, but you do have a very bad sprain. I am going to wrap it with an ace bandage and give you some pain medicine and an antibiotic to fill. You're going to need crutches for a few days, too. I want you to stay off it for at least a week, or you'll risk making it worse than it is now."

"I can't walk for a whole week?"

"If you want this to eventually turn into a long-term injury, then you're more than welcome to try walking, but you'll get back to your regular routine after you let it heal. I'll give you a note for work, but you'll also need to follow up in two weeks with the orthopedic clinic upstairs. Continue to use the ice packs. That was a smart move to use. It helped the swelling from being a lot worse than it is."

"Thanks," she said. She wasn't an eye-roller, but she couldn't help the motion as the doctor basically commended the guy who had cause her to fall in the first place. "Can I go now?"

"Yes. Your boyfriend is waiting out there for you now?"

"Boyfriend?" It took her a minute to realize he was referring to Andrei. "He's not my boyfriend." The doctor nodded with disinterest as he wrote down notes in her chart. He probably had a lot more patients to see.

"Don't forget. Keep weight off that ankle."

She nodded at him. He walked out of the room. She tossed her head back and closed her eyes, praying for strength. The day was turning into one of the longest days ever.

CHAPTER 4

ANDREI

THE NURSE HAD ASKED Andrei if he was Victoria's boyfriend, and he'd simply said yes. Andrei figured that would keep them from shooing him away, since he wasn't a friend or family. He didn't really have the right to be here, but he figured that he was the only person she had at the moment. Until he knew she was safe and taken care of, he wouldn't leave her.

She'd came out of nowhere in the courthouse, and now he felt like he at least owed her for playing a part in here being there. He'd already called his father and updated him on the case. Now, he had the rest of the afternoon free, so he stayed there waiting for Victoria.

She didn't seem too happy when they wheeled her

out from the back, so he didn't say anything about the boyfriend comment. The woman was probably still in some pain to.

He carried her out to the car in the wheelchair. "Should I take you home now?"

"Yes," she said. She gave him directions to her building and sat back as he drove her given route.

"Do you have someone to help you at home?" he asked.

"No, it's just me," she said. "I'll be okay. It's not like I have any stairs in my apartment. I'm on the first floor."

"Well, I am going to give you my number, so you can call me if you need anything," he said.

"That's not necessary."

"I know, but I'm giving it to you anyway. If you need anything, just call me on my cell number."

"Thank you," Victoria said, "but I'm pretty sure we can get in trouble for this.

"For exchanging numbers?"

"We are rivals in the courtroom. I doubt we're allowed to socialize outside of there. It's not professional."

"There is no hard rule to say we can't talk outside of court. Lawyers do it all the time. In fact, some lawyers are friends with prosecutors."

"I know that, but for me. It's a matter of ethics. I don't want to lose my job."

"Technically, our case is over, so there's nothing to keep you from going out with me."

"Going out with you?"

"That is what we're talking about, isn't it?"

"No! I meant socializing as friends."

"Oh? Cause it sounds like you were arguing against going out together, which I think is a big mistake."

"Really? A big mistake?"

This time he helped her out of the car, he at least gave her some dignity of hopping on her good foot while he took the pressure off the injured foot. He thought she would hit him if he lifted her up again.

"I can be very charming when I'm not knocking women out in hallways," he said.

She tried not to laugh, but she failed miserably. She looked less stressed out as he helped her through her building. The pain pills must have been kicking in. She smiled and looked a little groggy.

"Does that laugh mean you'll have dinner with me?" he asked as they neared her apartment. "One dinner to make up for the trouble I've caused, and then you'll never have to see me again. Promise."

She unlocked her door and hopped into her apartment. He gave her a long stare, and then he asked again for good measure.

"A fancy dinner will take your mind off that ankle, so what do you say?"

She looked like she was done putting up a fight. "Fine, but you will have to wait until my ankle is better before I can go anywhere. The doctor said I have to stay off it for a week."

"One week isn't a bad thing when I have something to look forward to."

"Do you ever let up on the charm?" she asked. She

was smiling at him, which took the sting out of her words.

"Not when it works, and you better call me if you need anything," he said. "I mean it."

"Yes, Mr. Rusak," she said, a teasing singsong in her voice.

He liked her when she wasn't so straight-laced and uptight. Getting to know her was going to be fun indeed.

"I like the sound of that," he said. "I may have to change my mind about you calling me Andrei."

She huffed. "Goodbye, Andrei." She couldn't slam the door, but she did shut it before he left. It didn't matter though, because he was holding her to that date.

He waited two days before he called her. He'd checked with her office, and she was indeed on sick leave. He had a feeling she wasn't going to call and ask for help, so he took the initiative and called her instead.

She picked up and he heard shuffling before she said anything. "Hello?"

"Victoria, it's Andrei."

"Oh, hi." She didn't sound like she was happy to hear from him, but she also wasn't openly hostile. He'd proceed cautiously.

"Is your ankle better?"

"It's still sore, but the pain pills and ice are definitely helping. Thanks for asking." she said.

"It sounded like you were having some trouble getting to the phone. Are you sure you're okay?" Andrei didn't want to be too nosy, but he wanted to help her if she needed anything.

"Yeah I was just trying to make dinner, but it's hard when you can't move around freely in your own kitchen."

"Then I called at the perfect time. I was just about to order dinner from my favorite Italian restaurant. I can swing by and bring you something."

"That's not necessary," she said. "I don't want to be a burden."

"You're actually on the way. Look, we can stay on the phone arguing about this, but I'm starving. Besides, I can hear your stomach crying out from here."

"You can't hear that!"

"I knew it. You're hungry."

"I'm starting to see why you won that case," she mumbled.

"Just let me do this for you."

She sighed. "Fine. You remember where I live?"

"Of course. I'll be there in an hour."

"Okay," she said.

After hanging up, he knew he was growing on her a little. Now, he was going to use this opportunity to turn that little into a damn lot.

He ran by Julio's and picked up his order. He made a second quick trip and bought some wine and pink roses before heading to her apartment.

When she answered the door, he nearly lost it. He'd only seen her a couple a days ago, but now in her jeans and sweater, she looked even more gorgeous. She looked soft and feminine. In her suit, she was a sexy lawyer with a reputation for fighting hard in the courtroom. In casual clothes, she looked soft and sweet, like the kind of woman you'd bring home to your mother.

"Are you coming in or not?" she asked.

"Yeah. Of course." He handed her the flowers. "These are for you."

"I thought we were just eating."

"We are."

"So you always just eat with flowers and wine?"

"If the mood strikes me, anything can happen."

"Anyone tell you how odd you are?"

"I've been called many things by my family, so I'm sure that's popped up once or twice."

The sound of her laughter filled the room, and it made him happy to have been the one to cause it.

"See? That wasn't too hard, was it?" He found

some glasses in her kitchen and a corkscrew as she sat on a bar stool.

"I laugh every now and then," she said.

"Good. I can't wait to hear more of it."

He watched her warm skin flush, and he wanted so bad to kiss it to see if it felt at hot as it looked. Instead, he pushed the longing down and popped open the wine.

"Don't worry about a thing," he said. "I bought everything we need. Do you want to eat in the living room and watch television?"

"That sounds like a plan." she said. "I actually have never eaten in the dining room or kitchen. It feels so impersonal."

"Me neither," he said. "It's either the living room or bedroom surrounded by stacks of papers."

She glanced up at him, as if surprised by his answer. "Exactly." She hobbled to the living room. He followed with the wine and food in hand. "Can you help me prop my leg up on this ottoman?"

"My pleasure," he said. "Is it okay to put the food on the coffee table?" he asked.

"Go for it. I've been eating in here because I can't seem to get comfortable anywhere else. The doctor said to keep it elevated to limit swelling, so I've been using this thing often. It makes me feel stiff, though."

"How about using a pillow and placing it in your back? That can help with the stiffness." he asked

"That actually sounds comfortable. Go into the closet in the hallway. I have extra pillows in there," she said.

He bought the pillows out, then he placed them in her back under her leg and under her arms.

"Wow, that feels amazing," she said, closing her eyes. "I should have called you over sooner."

"I told you. I'm here to help." Andrei smiled down at her.

"First the ice packs, now this. You sure you're a lawyer?"

"I played football in school. You get a lot of injuries and you learn how to help them fast."

"So you're a jock?"

"Far from it. It was rare if I ever got up off the bench." He passed her a glass of wine. "My father went to Columbia, so I went to Columbia. He played football, so I played football."

"Ah, so you're one of those."

"One of what?"

"Daddy's perfect son."

It was his turn to laugh. "I think he'd disagree with you there. I'm far from perfect."

"Really? You did go into law just like him. Now, you're working at his law firm. I'm almost positive that makes you perfect in his image."

"Kicking and screaming while doing it. Let's just say it wasn't as smooth sailing as you make it out to be."

"Okay," she said as she took a sip of her wine.

He watched her lips take in the red liquid, and he

got lost in her mouth. Those lips were plump and begging for him to kiss her.

Andrei turned to the side, so she wouldn't see the bulge that was slowly filling his pants. He focused on opening the dinner boxes as she got lost in television.

The local news was on.

"Damn it!" she shouted.

"What is it?" he asked, following her stare into the television.

"That guy right there! Vladimir Stavenoff." A man in a fancy suit walked into the courthouse with news people following him. "I was supposed to be the one to prosecute him. He's heavily involved with the Russian mob, and he was supposed to be my big case. Now I'm stuck here."

Andrei thought the man looked familiar, but he couldn't remember where he'd met him.

Victoria shifted in her seat. "Ow! My ankle."

Andrei was there in an instant to adjust her pillow and help her rotate her foot to a better position.

"Thanks," she said. "That was supposed to be my big case this week, and now my boss handed it over to someone else. I hate this."

He took her foot and rubbed away the tension without moving her ankle.

She was quiet as he worked, but she didn't object, so he kept rubbing her foot. Her skin was soft under his fingers.

"That feels...amazing."

"Good," he said as he worked the area above her ankle, loosening the muscles around her injury.

"I need to keep you here all the time," she said.

"Okay," he said as he continued to massage her calf.

"What do you mean okay?" she asked.

"I don't mind staying here to help you. Just say the word, and I'll stay."

"That's ridiculous."

"You just said—"

"I was just thinking out loud."

"Look, it's no big deal. You have a spare bedroom or something right?"

"Yeah."

"I can sleep in there for a bit, help you around here until you're well enough to go back to work. You actually live closer to the courthouse than I do, so it may help me out to be closer for my next few cases."

"You know how crazy that sounds, right?"

"Not if I make it worth your time."

"What does that mean?"

"You just said you feel stuck here while your work is being done by others. What if I gave you some of my resources to help you?"

"Isn't that a conflict of interest? If not, it should be."

"As long I and my firm don't represent the people you're fighting, it has nothing to do with us. Therefore it can't be a conflict of interest."

"I don't know." She sounded like she was on the verge of saying no.

"Just think of me as your assistant. I'm here to help for the next week or so until you can get back to doing things on your own, okay? I won't be any trouble and only help when you need me. You can keep your independence around here and use me when you need to."

"I'll admit you've got me curious about these resources," she said.

"Then it's settled," he said.

"I didn't say yes."

"But you want to, so I'm agreeing before you have to. That way, if anyone asks, you can say you had no part in it."

"Even when you say it like that, it sounds sketchy."

"Don't worry. I'll take good care of you." Andrei was a man of his word. Plus, he couldn't leave her like that. He wanted to spend time with her, and the perfect opportunity presented itself. Who was he to turn it down?

After dinner, he went home to pack some clothes and his paperwork for court. On the way back to her place, he did a little grocery shopping for breakfast, lunch, and dinner. He bought some sirloin steak and fish along with deli meat, vegetables for salad, and fruit. He tried to get various things in case he got something she didn't like.

He returned and raided her fridge. "You have nothing here," he said.

"I'm a takeout girl," she said.

He started putting food away. "I'll remember that."

"Did you really shop for groceries?"

"Yeah. That's what most people do. Except you, from what I'm hearing."

"Did you buy enough for an army or something? Are we having a party?"

"I didn't know what you liked, so I got a little bit of everything."

"At least we'll be ready for the zombie apocalypse," she said, picking up a few things he hadn't put away yet.

"Or world hunger, whichever hits us first. I'm making some ham and cheese, tuna fish, and chicken salad sandwiches for tomorrow. You may not need them all, but if you get hungry while I'm gone, you can just grab one. I also got you some salads, but I bought three different salad dressings in case you don't like one or two."

"I may surprise you and eat everything," she teased.

"Good. I like a woman with a healthy appetite."

She bit her lip, and he wanted nothing more than to bite it for her.

"I'll make breakfast before I go to work and put the beef in the crock pot with onions and peppers for dinner," he said. "Will you be able to manage if I set everything up for you?"

"Yes, Andrei, but this is too much. I didn't expect you to be a chef or anything. I can order delivery. Believe me, I have close personal relationships with all the delivery men in a four-block radius."

"It's no problem. I love cooking. It relaxes me before I have to work with the New York's crazies."

"Medical knowledge and a cook," she said. "I

swear, if you start cleaning my apartment, I'm going to beat you with my crutch."

"You can skip the crutch violence, because I don't clean."

"Thank God. I was starting to think you were too perfect."

"Perfection and I don't get along well at all."

"Good to know," she said. "And thanks for the help."

"You are welcome. Want me help you to your room? I'm going to call it a night soon, since I have an early case to prepare for."

"No, I am good. Goodnight."

"Goodnight, Victoria."

CHAPTER 5

VICTORIA

MAYBE VICTORIA WAS the one who needed a psych evaluation, because she didn't recognize herself. She'd gone from all business to allowing Andrei to room with her to getting excited about her date with him. It made no sense, but she was starting to realize whenever he was near, she couldn't think properly.

And those hands of his? Rawr. The man knew how to heal with them. He made her wonder what else he could do well with them.

That night, she couldn't sleep knowing he was in the next room. She tossed and turned until she had knocked most of the covers and a pillow off of the bed.

There was one way she knew would put her right to sleep, but she was pretty sure Andrei would hear her vibrator. Usually, it was just her, so the sound wasn't a problem. Now, she wished she'd gone with that silent version, even if it was slightly less powerful.

But she didn't need a vibrator when she could use her hands. She closed her eyes and imagined her hands were his, the same hands that felt so good on her bare skin.

Her hands roamed over her covered breasts, and she could feel her nipples harden as they pressed against her shirt. She gasped as she pinched her nipple, letting it harden underneath her touch.

Behind her closed eyes, she saw Andrei's smile and heard his deep, smooth voice as it flowed through her. She pinched her other nipple as her other hand traveled down over her stomach and into her pants.

Thinking about him already had her wet as she made contact with her warmth. She imagined it was his fingers exploring her, touching her in the most intimate way possible. She was going crazy with need, her back arching.

Her fingers circled her clit as she arched off the bed. In her mind, he was there kissing her and licking her until she could barely stand it. Her walls contracted as she ground into her sheets and covered her face to stifle her moans.

She imagined his butt in that bespoke suit of his. How she could see the outline of him. She thought of peeling off each layer like a sweet orange and wondered if he would taste sweet on her tongue.

Never had she fantasized about a guy like this, but none of that mattered as she cried out her release into her comforter and exploded from her orgasm. It was his face she saw as she came and came some more.

Part of her wondered if she was quiet enough to keep him from hearing, but as sleep took over her body, that was the last thing from her mind.

———

She woke up to the sound of a blender churning.

Morning light snuck through her windows, and she could hear Andrei in her kitchen.

That last night had given her the best sleep she'd had in weeks. She giggled and wondered if she should thank him for it. She blushed a little and decided against it.

The smell of fresh coffee lured her into the kitchen. He didn't see her right away, so she watched him from her bedroom doorway. His sleeves were pushed up, so she could see tattoos on his muscular forearms, which flexed as he cooked. There were intricate symbols and designs, and she wanted to see how far up they went, but his sleeves covered the upper part of them. He moved around her kitchen as if he'd been in it a thousand times, and she was happy that someone finally got to use the space properly.

She moved into the kitchen and saw boiled eggs, fresh fruit, and buttered toast. It was the pot of coffee that grabbed her attention.

"Good morning," he said, finally seeing her. "I have breakfast all set."

"I see that," she said, grabbing a pot of coffee and pouring some milk. "How long have you been up?"

"A few hours, but this was nothing,"

She grabbed a piece of toast and buttered it. "You're going to spoil me this way. I'm not sure if that's a good thing or not." She took a bite of her toast, and he just stared at her.

"Oh, it's a good thing for both of us," he said. He took her hand and took a bite of the toast she was holding. He chewed slowly and deliberately, savoring the butter, making it hard for her to do anything but watch him.

"Don't forget to swallow," he said.

She realized he meant her toast, so she swallowed it down.

That smile he gave her was making her all kinds of stupid, which might have bugged the hell out of her. Instead, it reminded her of what she imagined his mouth doing to her only hours before.

"If you need anything else let me know. I am have dinner on low in the crock pot with some potatoes, onions, and peppers. I'm off to work. I'll call to check in on you when I get a chance."

"You don't have to do that," she said. "I'll be fine."

He moved up to her so she had to crane her neck to stare up at him as he spoke. "I'm calling you, and you're going to answer. If you don't, I'll just race over here and do it in person."

"Okay," she said. "I'll answer."

"Promise me, or I may have to punish you for not following orders."

Punish her? Say what? "Look, I appreciate your help, but I'll be damned if I let you—"

She didn't have time to react. He captured her mouth in a second, a moment still too long for her brain to comprehend what was happening. His lips were slightly rough but still soft.

Her head was empty of anything but him, that kiss, and the warmth in her stomach. Then his tongue invaded her mouth until she thought she'd fall off her stool. His hand wrapped around her back, preventing that from ever happening. Instead, he pushed her closer to him, so she had to use her hands and place them on his chest.

Hell, that man could really kiss. She was so into it that he shocked her when he pulled away abruptly.

His fingers gently traced her swollen lips. "Answer the phone when I call, Victoria, or I will come back here."

The dominant sternness in his voice sent a chill over her that also made her body thrum to life. Her body was aware of every hard part of him, even the bulge that had pressed into her. He was most definitely excited, and she was right there with him, though she would never admit it.

"Fine," she said. "I'll answer."

"Good," he said. He kissed her again, but this time it was a quick peck on the mouth. "Do as I ask and I may have something tonight that will make you feel better." He winked at her, a half smile on his lips.

"Like what?"

"You'll find out later, but that's up to you."

She shook her head when he grabbed his briefcase and went out the door. He left her staring after him, a little bewildered.

It was almost pointless to try to get any work done. Andrei was in her head with every report she read and every briefing she tried to catch up on.

Being so distracted wasn't her at all. She didn't get giddy over men or anxious about seeing them again. Most women she knew, even her friends at work, cared about guys. Did they giggle and gossip about them? Sure.

Her? Nope. She didn't get butterflies and giggle.

She thought about seeing what Andrei was like frustrated. A few hours after he left, he called her, just like he said he would. She contemplated not answering when she saw his number on her phone, but she wanted to hear his voice too badly to hold out.

"I'm answering," she said. "Just as requested."

"I hear," he said. "That means I get to reward you. I'll be done in four hours. You may want to find something nice to wear."

"I thought we were having dinner here."

"Change of plans. I'm cashing in on that date you owe me."

"Oh, really?"

"Yes, and I think you're going to enjoy it. I'll see you in a few hours."

"I'll be here."

Victoria felt a case of nerves surge through her. She had spent most of the day fantasizing about hugging, caressing, and kissing him, thinking about his mouth. It was not like her to let her imagination run wild. She was trying to decide if she liked the way Andrei was making her feel.

The man was full of contradictions. He was kind and sweet when it came to taking care of her, but he also had an edge that she didn't understand just yet.

When she knew that she couldn't work anymore, she closed her laptop. She took a nice hot shower in her favorite lavender-scented bath gel, which always had the ability to relax her body and mind. She followed that with some bath oil and perfume.

As she got ready, she felt like a giddy school girl going out for the first time. It had been ages since she last had a date. Her workload had become so heavy that there was very little time for pleasure or fun. She didn't put herself out there very often. However, this man was very different from others she'd been around. Many men she dated were intimidated by her position as a prosecutor. Others wanted her to go all dominatrix on them. She could never find a balance between her work life and her personal life.

Andrei, however, had gotten under her skin. When he looked at her, she got goose bumps. Her heart rate increased uncontrollably when she thought of him, and her thoughts seemed to always turn sexual in one way or another until she could almost feel him inside of her, pushing inside of her.

As she thought about him and thought about the way he had kissed her like a man possessed, she could feel the wetness returning, warmth spreading between her thighs. Multiple times, she had to shake herself to clear her head and get ready for her date.

She remembered a cute little black dress she had in

the back of the closet. It was made of a soft flexible material with an empire waist and a plunging low bust line. With the length coming down to her thighs, it was too short for court, but perfect for a night out or, in this case, in. She finished with a multicolored pattern pashmina, throwing over her arms.

Suddenly the phone rang, and she raced to answer it, pulling her pashmina close.

"Hey!" she said, feeling relaxed and happier than she had any right to be, with her ankle.

"Are you feeling up for going out for my surprise?"

"Yes."

"Okay, I'm heading back. Pack an overnight bag."

"An overnight bag? Where are we going?"

"If I told you, it wouldn't be a surprise. Trust me. I'll make all the arrangements for our weekend date. You need to get out of the house, and I'm the one taking you."

"I remember agreeing to dinner. Not a weekend date."

"Have I given you any reason not to trust me?"

"No, I guess not."

"Good. I'll be there at six to sweep you away."

Victoria put the crockpot meal in the refrigerator and then packed her overnight bag. She grabbed all the essentials: her makeup bag, deodorant, her fancy underwear, her perfume, and a couple of extra outfits. She wasn't sure if she needed a bathing suit or not, so she threw that in her bag along with a towel, too.

After she finished packing, applying her makeup, and fixing her hair, she heard the key rattle as he stuck it in the door and came in.

She went out to meet him, and her heart was pounding and her stomach was a quivering just thinking about the handsome man coming in to take her out on this surprise trip.

He had changed since that morning. He wore a more casual top and pants which emphasized his height and musculature. His blue eyes seemed to sparkle as he took her in.

"Hello, beautiful," he said. He pulled a bouquet of

lilies with baby's breath from behind his back along with a box of fancy chocolate. "These are for you."

"Thank you," she said, taking her gifts.

He leaned forward and kissed her lightly on the lips. Before he could pull away, she held onto him a little longer. If she had her way, they would stay right there instead of going out. She wanted to take him to her bedroom.

"We don't have to go anywhere tonight," she said. "We could stay in." She leaned in to kiss him, but he dodged her.

"Oh, no. I have too much planned for us not to take advantage. I promise you're going to enjoy it. Are you ready to go?" he asked.

"Yes, I am ready. Let's go," she said.

She wasn't expecting him literally sweep her off of her feet.

"I am going to make sure your feet never touch the ground," he said.

"That sounds like a lot of work," she said, laughing as he maneuvered her through the doorway.

"You're definitely worth it though," he said.

As silly as it sounded, he had her grinning like a fool, a big smile spreading across her face. She didn't know the last time that she'd felt like this.

A limo waited for them downstairs. True to his word, Andrei didn't set her down until she was in the car.

He moved in next to her and wrapped his arm around her. "We are ready," he said to the driver.

"So where are we going exactly?"

"My father's law firm has a jet that we rarely get to use. I thought it would be romantic if we fly down to Montego Bay, Jamaica and spend the weekend. We can have separate rooms if you like, but I think after the last couple of days, we both could use time away from the city."

"That's extravagant," she said.

"Yeah, but you'll love it. It's beautiful this time of year," Andrei said.

"All right. It sounds like fun." Victoria said. Her thoughts conflicted in her head. She barely knew this man, but she was willing to go away with him. None of this was usual for her. "Lord, don't let me lose my job for dating a defense attorney," she thought. It wasn't exactly against the rules, but the ethical scandal of dating an attorney she'd gone up against was still there. Feeling him so close to her, he was too fine for any woman with a working sex drive to resist. She felt like she was being ripped apart, pulled in two directions.

They were only leaving for the weekend. She could think about reality when she got back. In that moment, she wanted to just get lost in him.

CHAPTER 6

VICTORIA

THEY HEADED to one of the nearby executive airports, one that was known for its exclusivity for the wealthy and a private airport that not many had access to. Teterboro was for posers who wanted to see and be seen. The plane was waiting on the tarmac for them.

She slid out only to have Andrei pick her back up.

"You don't have to carry me everywhere, you know," she said. "I'm not in as much pain anymore."

"Hush and let me do this," he said as he carried her up the steps. "Besides, I can think of a lot more fun things you can do with that mouth besides arguing."

"Oh, really?" she asked.

He captured her lips for a brief kiss. "Absolutely."

They entered the luxurious cabin with pure leather in butterscotch coloring with beige carpet. She sank down into the plush chair near the front of the plane where they were served red wine, cheese, and crackers.

Andrei's eyes roamed over her like he thought she looked good enough to eat, and she thought about taking him up on that penetrative gaze. She was glad she'd chosen the black dress that accentuated every part of her. Even from where she sat, she could tell that he was excited to be around her, and that made her a little more confident than she might be normally.

"Wine?" he asked

"Yes, please." He poured her a glass and then filled his own.

"Since we have some time, we might as well use it wisely," she said.

"And how do you propose we do that?"

"Talking. A very old pastime and something we lawyers do well. I became a lawyer because I love to talk and argue."

"That's true. We can talk our way through anything."

"So you first. Are you from New York?"

"Yes," Andrei said. "We're New Yorkers through and through. The Rusak Law Firm has actually been in my family for generations. First, my grandfather started it, when he didn't have much. Then my two uncles came on board followed by my dad. I actually wanted to be a doctor."

"Now that makes sense," she said, taking a bite of salty cheese.

"Maybe I would have too, but my dad kept nudging me until I finally came over to his side. My mother and sister are both doctors, so it wouldn't have been that uncommon. I'm sure you've have heard of the Rusak Maternal Clinic on the east side?"

"Of course. They're known as some of the best OB-GYNs in New York. That's your mother's place?"

"Mother and sister, actually. They do pretty well

for themselves. That's one thing Rusaks are good at. We follow others into our profession." He sounded a little bitter about that, but she didn't push him. It sounded like he was still angry about being railroaded into becoming a lawyer.

They sat there together sipping wine, smiling at one another.

"What about your family?"

"I grew up in California."

"That's right," he said. "Graduated from Stanford Law at the top of your class then moved to New York. After ten years of winning several high profile murder cases, you were finally offered an Assistant District Attorney's position of New York City."

"Sounds like you did your opposition research," she said.

"Would you respect me if I didn't?"

"Point taken. I tried to do the private law firm thing defending clients with Barnes, Keswick, Helsinki and Smitt for ten years, but I didn't enjoy it. I didn't know then that prestigious law firm meant pretentious clients. Most of mine were assholes."

"I can tell you right now, that's still accurate. Asses aplenty as clientele."

"Are you saying Vasin wasn't an easy client to work with?"

Andrei held his hands up. "I plead the fifth."

"You're definitely a lawyer."

"So how did you get the name 'Pitbull Bellamy?'"

"Not by choice, that's for sure. The other lawyers in the state nicknamed me that because they said I was vicious when it came to my work."

"You're tough, that's for sure. But vicious? I don't see that."

"Why not?"

"I've worked with vicious people...sometimes for them. Trust me, once you meet them, you'd never see yourself that way."

Victoria was grateful for people seeing her as a hard-ass in her profession, because it meant very few people messed with her. In her life outside of work, she still thought of herself as a kind, affectionate, fun-loving, and adventurous person. Victoria was had done well for a woman in her early thirties. Now if her parents would stop pestering her to have a child, she'd be good. Her mother mentioned it every time they spoke.

"Do you miss California?"

"Sometimes. I loved the weather there. The people were definitely kinder sometimes. Many more into odd things here and there, but that's California for you."

"You have siblings?"

"I have one sister and one brother, both are younger than me. My sister is a Registered Nurse, and my brother is a student at the University of California at Berkeley."

It took less than four hours to fly to Montego Bay, and at some point, Victoria had drifted off to sleep. She woke up in the best way possible. Andrei kissed her awake with light butterfly kisses.

"Hey, we're here," Andrei said. He lifted her up,

and she wrapped her arms around his neck as lifted her. By the time they got to the car, she was wide awake.

Night had fallen, and the lights around them gave off a romantic glow to the skyline and the water surrounding them. Some exclusive restaurants on the beach had their romantic sensual lighting displayed.

They pulled up to a place called Golden Lobster. She realized they were expected when she spotted a private table placed on the beach and a Caribbean band playing romantic music. A lobster dinner awaited them along with mash potatoes with lobster bits in it, a kale salad, and cold Chardonnay.

"You've really outdone yourself, haven't you?" she asked him as he sat her down.

"You tell me."

The band started playing soft Caribbean music, which surrounded them without being overwhelming.

"For a first date? Definitely outdone yourself."

"Is that a good thing?" he asked.

"Check with me at the end and maybe I'll tell you."

The waiter came out and filled their glasses with wine. Already, the stuff was going to her head and warming up other places. She ate and drank until horniness outweighed her tipsiness.

Of course that's when the man asked her to dance.

"Sprained ankle, remember?"

"Oh, I remember." He lifted her up in his arms and twirled her around, keeping her close. She laughed and felt her body relax against him. He danced with her in his arms until her head spun and the restaurant got ready to close, people slowly vanishing.

Andrei was holding her so tight that she could hardly breathe, but she still reveled in his nearness and the warm masculine scent that invaded her senses. He smelled like old spices mixed with the ocean, a smell she could easily get addicted to.

She guessed it was a good thing that he held onto her so well because she was so tipsy that she probably would have fallen on the floor if he'd let her go, especially since she couldn't put weight on her ankle.

He finally slid her down the length of his body, but he still held her up so her feet never touched the ground. She could feel the hardness of him pressing against her stomach as she linked her arms around his neck.

They ground into each other as they swayed, long after the music stopped playing and the band dispersed. He felt so damn good that she forgot everything around them. She shivered, and it wasn't from the weather. She knew that he wanted her, and she needed to let him know she felt the same way. He leaned down and kissed her neck, which made fire burst right where he kissed her.

That's when she whispered softly, "I want you." He placed his arms around her and lifted her back up and walked down the beach.

The hotel wasn't far from the restaurant. The Flying Eagle Resort had the honeymoon suite for them.

"Why are we in the honeymoon suite?"

"Because that was the only one available."

Victoria raised her eyebrows. "Are you sure about that? Didn't you offer to let us have separate rooms?"

"I thought that you might enjoy being in the same room as me tonight. I can make it worth your while."

"A little presumptuous of you," Victoria said.

"A guy can dream," he said.

The room was fit for royalty, trimmed in gold and white with billowing satin curtains and bed attire to match. They had a large canopy bed with large bed post and plush carpet that had her feet sinking into it.

"Kiss me," he demanded, and she didn't disappoint him.

She kissed him until all she could taste was him on her tongue. Heated need filled her. She allowed him to consume her, hungry tongue and warm hands.

His fingers teased the edge of her dress and lifted it

above her head. He moved them over to the huge king-sized bed until she sat on the soft bedding. She kissed his sexy lips and sucked them as his tongue teased hers. He slid his lips from her mouth down to her neck as she moaned with pleasure. She could feel chills up and down her spine as he nibbled and caressed her neck.

She moved back to the center of the bed and watched as Andrei got naked. She made a mental note to do that herself next time. He was even hotter than she thought. The tattoos on his arms swirled up and over his chest and around his nipples.

Each muscle on his abs was defined, making her fingers itch to touch him. When he finally undid his pants, she was on edge. As he slid his boxers down, his hardness jutted out from the constraints.

He crawled up her body, kissing his way up. His hand slid up her back and unlatched her bra, allowing her breasts to be completely exposed to him.

"So lovely," Andrei said, staring at her bare breasts before he opened his mouth and licked and sucked her nipple as he caressed the other breast with his hand.

She moved closer to him, feeling her sensitive nipples hardening at his attentions. Andrei's excitement intensified, and she could feel him bulging against her thigh. The feeling only pushed her arousal up to another level, until she felt her moisture pool in her panties.

As if sensing her excitement, his fingers found her covered mound and laced inside, letting the evidence coat his fingers.

"I want to taste you," he said. The burning heat in his eyes almost undid her. He slid down until he faced her covered pussy. His fingers slid under the band and pulled her last remaining piece of clothing down until she was bare for him.

Her clit throbbed and ached for his touch. He began to lick at her as if she was tasty, sweet nectar for him to devour. When he found her clit, he sucked it, making her head spin and sending sensational waves through her entire body. He initiated an endless orgasmic wave, and she had to hold on to the bed to keep her balance.

She threaded her fingers through his hair as he ate at her. All of her control was shattered as she involuntarily thrusted her hips up and down. He broke her until she felt her wetness pouring out of her. He didn't let a single drop of her go to waste as his mouth lapped at her.

Although she didn't know how much more she had left to give, he wasn't finished with her. He opened his mouth and continued to massage her clit with his tongue and gently sucked on it. He inserted his finger deep into her vagina as blast after blast over pleasure hit her. No man had ever worked her body as expertly as he did.

She didn't know when he'd removed his underwear, but she felt him hot and ready at her entrance

"Fuck," he said.

"What?" she asked, barely holding on. If he didn't hurry, she was going to go crazy.

"No protection."

"I don't care. Please, Andrei."

She could tell she'd broken down any resolve he'd had to stop, and she didn't want him to ever stop.

He raised himself up to position himself. Victoria could see that he was extremely large, maybe the largest guy she'd ever been with, as pre-cum dripped from the tip. When he finally entered her, she bucked her hips up to meet his thrust, even though he felt almost too big for her. Her inner walls gripped him tight, afraid to let him leave her. When he did, he pushed farther into her then before.

Her muscles gripped his penis and worked him like he was a wild animal. He was crazed with pleasure. He began to bite her on one shoulder. She met him with her own roughness as she scratched and clawed down his back. He moaned and cried out as Victoria took him for all he was worth and then some, neither one of them holding back as they met thrust for thrust.

She reveled in the pleasure as his enormous cock touched all of her sensitive spots and stretched her to her most delightful limits. He switched angles, hitting her G-spot and stimulating sensitive spots she never knew existed before him.

"Close," he panted. "So close."

"Yes," she cried, locking her legs around his waist.

The tempo of their thrusting accelerated, until they both burst into a massive orgasm. She shut her eyes and let the pleasure consumer her inside and out. His groan let out as he released deep within her, filling her up. Their sounds of lovemaking echoed in the room around them until they both came down from their high.

CHAPTER 7

ANDREI

ANDREI HAD DONE some crazy things in his life, but running into Victoria was one of the best accidents to ever happen to him.

She was the perfect mixture of strong and sweet, confident and sensitive, that it made him shiver with excitement all over again. Lying in that bed with her in his arms, he felt in his heart that he had received a perfect dark-haired angel. Which meant he was going to the deepest parts of hell for lying to her. Sure, it was a lie by omission, but she wouldn't see it that way. When was a good time to tell her he was divorced with two kids? Definitely not when he moved in to help her. Certainly not last night.

If he was honest, he should have told her when they talked about family on the plane ride there.

He should have at least given her a choice before they got in too deep, but he wasn't a good man. He had demons and a past, plus two kids who were a big part of his life.

The last thing he wanted was to scare her away, so he figured he had better wait until he knew her better. There was really not much to getting to know after the night he had with her.

Sunlight filled their room, and he loved the way she looked snuggled close to him. Her cocoa brown skin looked good enough to eat, and her curves were enough to somehow suck all the oxygen out of the room. Even as he thought of her sweet taste on his tongue, he got hard for her.

He'd never wanted anyone the way he wanted her.

She moved against him and those light grey-brown eyes fluttered open.

"Morning," he said, putting a hand behind her head and giving her a long kiss.

"Good morning," she said. "What time is it?"

"We're on an island and on no one's time clock, so it's whatever you want it to be."

"So what? No amazing breakfast to wake up to?"

"After last night, you're lucky I'm even alive. I can't believe that I'm awake enough to talk to you. Anyone ever tell you that you can knock a guy out with your sexy self?"

"Not my sexy self, but my courtroom self is another matter entirely."

He laughed softly before kissing her cheek with the lightest touch. "Well, either way, I'm happy to be at your mercy. If you're hungry, we still have the dessert we never got to last night."

"What dessert?"

He nodded to the nightstand beside them. "I had strawberries, chocolate, and whipped cream brought in before we arrived, but we were a little too occupied."

"Well, I'm not one to let good fruit and dessert go to waste." She reached over him and grabbed a strawberry, which already had the tops cut off. She bit part of it, and he grabbed the remainder from her fingers with his teeth. He took each finger and sucked the sweet strawberry juice off, using his tongue to get every bit of it. Her breath caught in her throat.

He took another and dipped it in the chocolate. He held it at a distance and made her work for it, keeping it tantalizing close but moving away every time that she could almost bite it. When her lips finally wrapped around the strawberry, he thought it was the sexiest thing he'd ever seen. He dipped a couple more in chocolate and covered it with whipped cream, but Victoria had other plans for the chocolate.

"It's my turn to taste you now," she said, her voice seductive and taunting. She straddled him and brought the chocolate closer. "I've wanted to trace my tongue over these intricate designs since I first saw them."

"Have you?" he asked.

"Uh, huh. And one thing you should know about me is that I always get what I want."

"I do, too, honey. So what do you suggest we do about that?"

"I think we need to come to a mutually beneficial agreement."

"And how does this agreement work out?"

"What's good for me is good for you and vice versa." She drizzled some chocolate over the tattoos that covered his chest. She leaned over and licked up the chocolate tracing his lines.

"I think I can work with that kind of arrangement," he said. Her teeth grazed his nipple. His breath hitched, and he held onto her as she used the chocolate to trace a pathway down his body.

He was fully erect now, and Victoria wrapped her hand around him.

"Victoria," he said. "Don't start something you can't finish."

"I always finish the things I start, Andrei. Always."

After he relaxed back onto the bed, she poured the chocolate all over his cock, using her wrist to make it circle around and around, and slowly licked it off.

"Fuck," he cried out. Her mouth felt so warm and

good around him, and he tried to keep from forcing her to take too much of him. She wouldn't let him hold anything back.

She sucked harder until he thrashed around with delight. His hands were in her hair as she began bobbing her head up and down, a slow and steady rhythm that drove him wild and made him clutch the sheets with his fists. She sucked and ran her tongue underneath the head. Then she took the whole length down her throat and sucked it so hard that the mixed pleasure and slight pain made him shout.

This woman was amazing, but she was going to kill him if she kept doing that. Her fingers danced at that sensitive area just under his balls.

"I'm coming, Victoria," he said, trying to warn her. She didn't move away. Instead, she sucked harder, milking him for all he was worth. He screamed as he came this time, but still she stayed there taking all of him.

"Damn, woman," he said. "You really know how to make a sound argument."

She laughed. "Did you ever doubt I could?"

"Not for one second."

"We'll have to return to New York tomorrow, but until then, I'm going to enjoy every inch of you." Andrei said. "Are you enjoying yourself so far?"

"Yes," Victoria said. "I think I needed this."

"Good. I'm glad you're into it."

Her hand explored his chest as they settled into the soft bed. The sheets were really rumpled, but they didn't care.

"Andrei, can I ask you something?"

"After what you just did, you can ask me anything you want."

"Have you ever dated a fellow lawyer before?"

The question took him back some.

"No, this is my first time," he said. "Does that bother you?"

"Not really," she said. "I just...want to make sure this isn't some weird kink for you or something. Having sex with the opposing counsel..."

He lifted her chin so she looked into his eyes. "I

promise you the last thing I would ever see you is some weird kink, Victoria."

She smiled back at him, so he kissed her. He could kiss her four hours and never get bored from it.

"What about you?" he asked. "Any guys who need to have their asses kicked? "

"No, you are my first. I tend to stay away from guys I might meet in a professional context." she said. "Why would they need their asses kicked?"

"Any man who lets you go would need one," he said.

"Maybe I'll take you up on that offer sometime." She dropped a kiss on his shoulder.

"I believe that this is the beginning of something special and real," Andrei said. "I don't want to ever let go of you." He wrapped his arms around her and gave her a kiss.

"Then don't," Victoria said.

Andrei began to tickle her until Victoria begged for mercy. He pulled her into his arms and brought her to the bathroom. They took a hot shower together in the high-tech shower stall. The warm water was endless, and they quickly soaped each other down, touching each other in intimate spots and kissing endlessly while the water sprayed them both.

Everything quickly turned into another lovemaking session. He couldn't keep his hands off her long enough for them to get anything remotely productive done. He couldn't get enough of her.

Victoria jumped up and wrapped her legs around his waist, and that was it. He reached down and guided his throbbing cock into her wetness, pinning her back against the wet tile as he surged inside of her body, taking her over and over again. He felt like he was on the verge of exploding into a thousand pieces. He'd never be able to get enough of her. When they'd cleaned themselves off a second time, they went back to bed holding each other while sharing a pillow, their faces so close together that their noses nearly touched.

They left Montego Bay early the next morning, and he hoped she'd never want him to leave her, especially after he finally came clean to her. If he didn't do it soon, their new relationship would be over before it could fully begin.

CHAPTER 8

VICTORIA

MONDAY MORNING CAME, and Victoria finally felt strong enough to go back to work. The week passed by slowly since she still wasn't able to go and present cases in the courtroom, but at least she was getting back into her old routine. That's what she needed.

As she typed, her thoughts drifted back to Andrei. His hands on her, his scorching kisses on her body, his tongue in her mouth. There were so many memories that made her feel a little wet, and she couldn't focus on any writing.

She set her writing work aside to focus on reading depositions for upcoming cases she'd be trying for the upcoming weeks.

It still didn't matter. Andrei was in her head, and he wasn't getting out anytime soon. Even if she tried harder, she doubted that she could get him off of her mind. Their vacation in Jamaica together had been passionate and perfect.

Deedee and Roslyn, her friends and coworkers, were both there her first day back waiting to hear all about her time away with a sprained ankle. They pounced on her at lunchtime, the two of them coming into her office for a joint attack.

"There's nothing much to talk about. I hurt my ankle and that's it."

"You know I saw you," Deedee said. She played with a strand of her hair and smirked at Victoria.

"Saw me what? What are you talking about?"

"In the courthouse with that guy touching all over your foot."

"He was just making sure the swelling went down."

"I'll bet he got a lot of swelling to go down," Roslyn teased.

"Shut up," Victoria said. "Someone else might hear you."

"No one else cares," Deedee said.

"Tell that to the interns."

Deedee sat on the edge of her desk. "So who was he?" The woman was like a dog with a very tasty bone. She wasn't letting it go.

Victoria blew out a breath. "Just a lawyer," Victoria said. She didn't know how much to share with them. Her relationship with Andrei was still new, and she wasn't ready to put it all out there for everyone else to analyze and judge. It was her relationship, and it was sort of iffy since it was so new. She could do whatever she wanted and with whomever she wanted. She was a grown woman, but she didn't want the gossip to spread around the office.

"You know what this means?" Rosalyn said.

"It means she's got a crush on Mr. Hot Lawyer."

She pulled her friends into her office and closed the door. "Fine. There may be something between us, but I don't want anyone else to know." She sighed.

"You owe me twenty-five dollars and a free lunch," Deedee said to Rosalyn.

"You two did not bet on me."

"We're paid shit for this job, Vic. Of course we bet on you," Rosalyn handed her money. "I'll buy you lunch tomorrow."

"What did you bet exactly?"

"Rosalyn said you wouldn't date a lawyer," Deedee said. "I bet that you would if you found one you liked who could handle you, so I win."

"Great friends, both of you."

"If it helps, we made it back when we first met you," Rosalyn said.

"That barely helps," Victoria said.

Deedee was the receptionist, and Rosalyn worked as a paralegal. Both welcomed Victoria as the newest Assistant District Attorney on her arrival, when so many others didn't give a damn about who she was. They were nicer than a lot of the lawyers that Victoria had to deal with.

Although Victoria was grateful for her friends, sometimes she felt that she couldn't talk to them the way she wanted to.

District Attorney Andrew Smith walked into her office just then.

"We'll see you for lunch," Rosalyn said, pulling Deedee out of the office with her. Victoria saw her mouth, "Ten minutes." They scurried out of her office.

"Ms. Bellamy, it's good to see you back here ready to work," her boss said.

"Yes, sir," she said. "I'm glad to be back."

"That's what I like to hear. You've been doing exceptionally well over the past few months. Keep it up, and I have no doubt your future here with us will continue to grow."

"Thank you, Mr. Smith. I appreciate that."

"I know you have to stay off that injury for a few

more days, but I came to offer you a special case since I knew you would want."

"What case?"

"The one against Vladimir Stavenoff."

Victoria sat up straighter in her chair, her eyes widening. "I thought he was already on trial. I saw him at the courthouse days ago when the press did a piece on him."

"That was postponed due to his ailing, elderly mother, or so he says."

"Of course." The man was a supposed family man, but he had been linked to shootings and human trafficking. However, no one could prove it. Before her injury, Victoria had been building a case on him so the man could finally be brought to justice.

"It starts up again in a few days, so I wanted to see if you want it."

"Yes," she said. "I absolutely want it."

"Good, because if anyone can put this guy away, it's Pitbull Bellamy. Am I wrong about that?

"No, sir. I definitely won't let you or the office

down." She straightened her shoulders and tried to look like she lived up to her reputation.

"Glad to hear it. Keep me posted with this one, since the media has already made it into a circus. The last thing we want is anything to go wrong with this one and for them to catch wind of it. Understood?"

"Yes, sir. Thank you for the opportunity."

"You've earned it. Now, bring him to justice."

Victoria had a date with Andrei that evening, but if she wanted to win this case, she needed to dive into it completely with no distractions. As much as she wanted to see Andrei, he was a distraction she didn't need. She decided to call him.

He picked up on the second ring. "Hey, beautiful," Andrei said.

"Hi," she said, hesitating.

"You okay? You don't sound too great."

"Listen, I can't make it tonight."

"That's all you're worried about? No problem. We can just reschedule for later this week."

"That's the thing. My boss just handed me a big case, and I'm not sure how long I'll be on it or when I'll be free anytime soon."

"Victoria, I'm not going anywhere. Take all the time you need. I understand."

She was quiet. Most of her past relationships suffered because she was too dedicated to her job, and now this guy was letting her do it without getting upset. Was he really into her? Either he respected her space or he didn't care very much. She hoped it was the former, not the latter.

"Thank you," she said. "I'll call you when I can."

"I'll look forward to it, beautiful."

Although he'd given her permission, she still felt guilty for bailing on him. What would that distance mean when or if they ever got back together?

She knew she'd done the right thing. He'd moved out of her place when they'd gotten back, since she was more able to move around, but they hadn't talked about what they were to each other now after Montego Bay, and she wasn't sure if that was a good thing or not.

———

Over the next few days, she focused on nothing but work and pushed Andrei to the back of her mind. He still popped up frequently in her thoughts, but she couldn't let that mess with her court game plan. Not if she wanted to win and see Vladimir Stavenoff get what he rightfully deserved.

Her first day for Vladimir Stavenoff's trial felt like déjà vu all over again. Judge Hughes presided over the court yet again. Victoria had done her research on Stavenoff's defense team, but she found out early that morning that he'd fired them and hired a new team to represent him. It was too soon to find out who his new hires were, but that night she was going to research every last person on that defense team.

She wasn't going to let anything stop her from winning this case. This was her redemption, a way to get back in the game, and no one was going to keep her from completing it. She came to win.

When Vladimir Stavenoff finally walked in with his new team, Victoria felt like the air had been sucked out of the room.

Andrei and his team stood next to Vladimir Stavenoff.

Why didn't she put the thought together after seeing Roman Vasin's name on the witness list? She was completely off her game, and it was all because of Andrei Rusak.

She gripped her chair's armrests so tightly that she thought she'd break them. He seemed just as surprised to see her too. Focus was her main thought. She had to focus, or she'd lose the case before she even gave her opening statement.

Same judge and same defense team. If there was a worse case scenario, she was in it and had no way out. She could feel the flames biting at her skin already, and if she wasn't careful, they would engulf her completely.

"All rise for the Honorable Judge William Hughes," the bailiff said. The people in the room stood before the judge came out and took a seat. "You may be seated."

Judge Hughes spoke, breaking Victoria out of her shock. "The prosecution will now present the case of Vladimir Stavenoff versus the People."

She rose and took a deep breath. "Your Honor, ladies and gentleman of the jury, I present the case of Vladimir Stavenoff, who has been accused of breaking and entering the residence of Mr. Vasin, stealing his gun and pick-up truck then using it to commit murder. The lab will submit evidence of the DNA ballistic report from the gun and finger prints found in the truck and in the business, which will all be submitted by the Crime Scene Investigation team of the state of New York." She sat down and waited for Andrei to speak.

"Your Honor, ladies and gentlemen of the jury," he said, "the prosecution would have you believe that my client broke in and entered the residence of Roman Vasin, stole a firearm and a truck all before committing murder. There is no proof that Vladimir broke into the house, stole the firearm, or stole the car, which I will prove in the duration of this case.

Victoria finally glanced over in his direction, and he met her gaze with one of confusion but determination. As the case continued, they both exchanged looks several times. Victoria could not stop looking at Andrei, remembering that special weekend with him only days before. Now, he was representing one of the most dangerous men in the city. As their eyes met again, Andrei smiled at her. It wasn't the full one she'd come to enjoy from him, but it was one that still made her hold her breath. A dull pain went through her, but she had to push it away. Apparently, she wasn't fast enough, because the judge noticed.

"Attorneys Bellamy and Rusak, approach the bench immediately!" The shock of the judge addressing them made her nervous as she walked up to him with Andrei.

They approached with horror in their eyes, because they both knew what he was going to say. There was no avoiding it now.

"What in the hell is going on here! Is there something you want to tell me?" He paused with cold fury in his eyes. "I...am...waiting."

What could they say that wouldn't get them thrown off the case? They both remained quiet instead of saying something they might regret later.

"Fine. Have it your way. I am advising both parties to assign another attorney to assume the responsibility of this case. I will be contacting each of your respective offices to ensure my recommendation is taken seriously. Is that understood?"

"Yes, Your Honor," they both aid at the same time.

"Court is dismissed until further notice," Judge Hughes said before banging his gavel. He looked at them both and said, "I'll see both of you in my office. Now!"

Victoria and Andrei sat as the judge paced in his chambers.

"I won't tolerate this behavior in my courtroom."

"What behavior, sir?" Andrei asked.

The judge snorted. "You know. You must find alternate attorneys for your replacements."

"We'll be happy to request a substitute for each of us, Your Honor," Andrei said.

Victoria shot him a look. Of course he'd be fine. This wasn't the case of a lifetime for him.

"Ms. Bellamy, do I have your word as well?"

"I'll do my best, Your Honor," she finally said.

"Oh, you'll need to do better than that if either of you hope to present in my courtroom again," Judge Hughes said. "What you're doing could be seen as ethically immoral for those in your position. I suggest you figure this out sooner rather than later. Now if you are kind enough to excuse me, I have a job to get done that doesn't involve personal matters. We're done here."

They left his chambers, and Andrei pulled her to the side. "We need to talk."

"I'm not in the mood right now, Andrei."

"We need to figure this out together. The sooner the better."

"Fine," she said. In her head she was slowly watching years of hard work flushing down a clogged drain, and it made her sick to her stomach thinking about it. A weekend fling was going to ruin everything.

"Dinner at my place tonight, and I won't accept no for an answer, Victoria."

"Okay. I'll be there. Can I go now?" She could hear the anger in her voice, but she was too angry to care.

"Go," he said. "But if you're not over at my place by eight, I'm coming to you. I still have a key."

She walked away before she could say anything else in the heated anger that filled her. What bothered her most was that she didn't know who she was angrier at, Andrei or herself. She had a headache.

CHAPTER 9

ANDREI

WHENEVER ANDREI WAS TROUBLED, he went to visit his longtime friend Erik. He always knew what to do. Although Erik wasn't book smart, the man had street smarts and sage advice to offer anyone who listened. The man loved to read, despite not having a traditional education.

Although Erik wasn't ever the smartest man in the room, Erik was like a therapist. The guy had read a lot of self-help and psychology books in his spare time, and he lived for solving people's problems — life-coaching had become a hobby.

They both had been so busy lately that they had not seen each other in a while, almost two weeks. Still, he'd called Erik and told him about Victoria.

Erik lived in one of the high rises on the other side of town. He could afford the place only because the owner also owned the bar below, where Erik was a bartender. They didn't see each other every day, but they were still close.

"Hey, man."

"Hey."

"Lunch?"

"Sounds good. When and where?"

"Seafood. Casper's. Twelve thirty."

"See you there." He hung up.

Andrei needed his friend's advice before he met Victoria that evening.

Erik arrived first, and he spotted Andrei as he came across the street.

"Andrei, over here, man." He raised his hand and beckoned to him. They had to stand in line, because it was a popular restaurant and always packed. "We have a fifteen minute wait. Is that all right with you?" Erik asked.

"Sure. That's fine. So, how have you been?"

Erik smiled. "Great. Life is always as great as you make it. How about you?"

Andrei laughed at his friend's philosophy. "Good. Could be better."

"Does that have anything to do with that new lady you've been talking about?"

"Maybe. How about you? You seeing anyone?"

Erik said. "No, man. Can't seem to find the right one."

One of the other customers sitting in the waiting room seemed to be listening to them, so Andrei nudged Erik, gestured to her, and shut up. They sat in companionable silence. The dinner line moved forward, and finally they were seated at a table.

"You've seen a lot of women since you divorced Trish. You've told me all about your one-night conquests, like that woman who could bend like a contortionist. You said that she was a crazy bunny boiler, though. You haven't bothered to hit it even twice in a while. So tell me about this Victoria," Erik said.

Andrei smiled. "She's amazing, a beautiful woman with intelligence to back it. I've never met anyone like her."

"Then what's the problem?" Erik asked.

Andrei answers "I don't know. I think our jobs are going to be a problem. She was in court this morning prosecuting a client of mine."

"Isn't that how you met?"

"Apparently, the court system wants us thrown together until we crash."

"Do you love her?" Erik asked.

"I don't know. It's kind of soon for that, isn't it?"

"Lawyers, some of the best bullshitters around, I swear."

"It's not bullshit."

"Trust me. If you love her, you'd know."

"You're an ass sometimes. You know that, right?"

"That's why you come to me for advice. I'm the ass who tells the truth, no bullshit."

They ordered the seafood platter with fish, oysters, crab, and shrimp. Andrei wasn't sure why they loved the place so much, since it was fancier than he liked with chandeliers, a Koi fish pond, and wallpaper with huge fishing boats in the ocean catching large hordes of fish, lobsters and oysters. There was even a large lobster hanging from the ceiling, caught in a fishing net.

When the food arrived, he was reminded of why he dealt with the pompous scenery. It smelled incredible, and the chef knew exactly the right spices to make the dishes come alive. He thought about Victoria and wondered if she'd like it there. She might enjoy the ambiance.

"Erik, what do you think about me dating a black female lawyer?" Andrei asked.

"I think it's beautiful, man. It's not about the race. No matter the shit people spit out these days. It's about the soul, the mind, the heart, and the love."

"Leave it to you to sound like a hippie. But it's not about her race...it's the possible professional implications if we're seeing each other," Andrei said.

"Are you happy?" Erik asked.

"Actually, for the first time in my life, I am happy," Andrei said.

"Well that's all that counts," said Erik. "True love is hard to find."

"There's just one thing. I haven't told her about Asya and Naida."

"You haven't told her about the kids? Man, that's all kinds of messed up. Stuff like that will mess with your karma."

"I know. I know. I want to tell her, but you should've seen the look she gave me in court today, like she was disappointed and angry at the same time. I fucking hated it."

"People fight. It may not be as bad as you think, but if you keep lying to her, that's going to blow up before you know it. It might be a lie of omission, but you need to tell her."

"That's what I'm worried about."

"You should trust her to accept that part of you.

Grab hold of this one and never let go. If she's as amazing as she sounds, it'll work itself out."

"You need to start charging for this. It's gold."

"I know, but bartending lets me impart my wisdom to the masses. I'm good with that."

"I'll have to bring her by one night, so you can meet her," Andrei said.

"I would love to meet her. Must be a spectacular woman to have you all worked up like this," Erik said.

"Yeah, she is."

After talking it over with Erik, Andrei knew that he had to give this relationship some serious thought. He knew that his life, career, and his eternal happiness would depend on the type of decisions that he made over the next few days.

Problems hit him as soon as he got back to the office. His father was there to greet him as soon as he got off the damn elevator.

"What the hell did you do now?" his father roared.

His father obviously didn't care that the staff heard him. They knew better than to stare though. Otherwise, they'd be in the receiving end of his anger.

Andrei refused to play. Not when he has so much on his mind already. He started walking to his office, hoping his father waited until they got there to have one of his blowouts. "I'm sure you'll tell me sooner or later."

"Judge Hughes called me. He wants someone else on the Stavenoff case. Are you involved with the ADA?"

"It's not what it looks like," he said. He closed the door after his father followed him into his office.

"Good because it looks like you're sleeping with the ADA and ruining this firm's reputation."

"That's all you see, but—"

"I will not have our reputation ruined just because you wanted to get your rocks off."

"Would you let me talk?! Her name is Victoria, and she's more than just someone I want to get my rocks off with. We didn't even know that we would be on the same case today."

"You expect me to believe that?"

"You're going to believe what you want to believe. I have no control over that. Never did. But believe me when I tell you that this is more than just some fling."

"I don't care what it is. You end it and you end it now, or you won't like the repercussions." His father didn't give him a chance to respond. Instead, he stormed out of his office and slammed the door shut.

His father had riled him up. He gripped the edge of his desk tightly to keep from running after the man and setting him straight, but he knew it wouldn't do any good. When his father made up his mind about something, he stayed that way. He was stubborn like a mule.

End it? He only had a few hours to go before he saw Victoria again, but his father made things more difficult. The last thing he ever want to do was hurt her, but maybe they both need a reality check about what their relationship meant for the careers and their futures.

CHAPTER 10

ANDREI

VICTORIA MET him at his place at seven thirty. He realized, oddly, that she didn't know where he lived, until he texted her his address after his encounter with his father. Of course he lived in a swanky high rise, but he made his place his own with interesting artwork that filled his walls and gave life to the dead space around the open area.

"Wine?" he asked her.

"Yes, please," she said.

"Dinner will be ready soon," he said, sitting on the couch. He'd gotten it from a meal service that just told him to pop it into the oven for 15 minutes before serving. He was grateful that she followed him into the living room. He wasn't enjoying the fact that she sat so far away from him, but he would go with whatever made her comfortable.

"We must figure this thing out, Victoria. Exactly where do we stand?"

Victoria took a deep breath. "I like you, Andrei. I really do. Honestly, I can't get you off my mind."

He grinned at her words. "Really?" He was going to say she invaded his thoughts, too, but he waited. He liked the fact that she thought about, and got him hard thinking about the fantasies that probably crossed her mind as much as he did his.

He moved closer to her, crowding her space. He wanted her to think of nothing but hum as she chose her next words carefully.

"This is insane," she said. "I can't do this if it's going to impact my work."

"Why do I hear a but in there?" He placed a hand on her bare knee and made circles on the smooth skin.

"My job is my life. I've worked hard to get where I am today. The last thing that I need is a distraction, and you distract the hell out of me."

His hands slid up her leg. "Sometimes distractions can be amazing."

"I thought you wanted to talk about us," she said. She shifted her weight like she might move away, but she didn't.

Already, he could hear the hesitation in her breath and almost feel the pulse in her thigh beating against his hand as he slid up farther. "That's what I said, but being this close to you has me changing my mind."

He took that moment to let his hand reach her covered pussy. She was wet and ready for him just like he thought she'd be. All thought of talking escaped him as he pushed her panties aside and stuck two fingers inside her.

She moaned. "Andrei."

"God, I love the way your beautiful skin flushes when you get excited like that." His thumb flicked her clit, and she moved forward, forcing his fingers in deeper. "We could turn this into an argument or a discussion. It doesn't matter, but one thing is certain. I'm going to fuck you tonight and make sure we both enjoy it."

He didn't wait for her to say anything to contradict him. He removed any chance of that by claiming those sweet, luscious lips of hers. Before any talk of what they were to each other happened, he wanted her to feel how much he wanted her, needed her.

He loved the way she opened up to him, making it easy for him to take control. He moved his fingers inside of her and found that special spot to make her moan even louder. In that moment, it didn't matter what anyone else thought or wanted them to do.

Fuck what was right or wrong, because he craved her more than anything or anyone. Andrei knew without a doubt that she wanted him. He could not get her out of his mind all day, and he'd be damned if he was going to let anyone take her away from him. He couldn't get enough of her. They hadn't been together in days, but it felt like weeks. Too fucking long. He had to be inside of her soon or he was going to go crazy.

Andrei lifted her up and carried her to his bed. He took his time removing her clothes she was an orange for him to peel. He had to get to the succulent fruit inside, no matter the cost. He caressed her tummy and moved up to cup her breast, so ripe that it filled his hand perfectly. He enjoyed her fingers roaming through his hair as he went down further to kiss her tempting opening that was just for him.

He used his tongue to find her clit, and when he did, the muscles in her thighs contracted around him. He could feel tremors going through her body as she arched her back and began to thrust against his tongue. He grabbed her hips with both hands to hold on and keep contact with her clit. She screamed with pleasure as her clit expanded enough for him to suck even harder on it.

His fingers found her luscious opening again as he continued to explore her clit and discover the addictive reactions she had from his attentions. He knew and she was coming, could sense it but a pending storm ready to explode. Her screams were endless as copious amounts of juices poured out of her. To Andrei, her taste was the sweetest thing he'd ever enjoyed, and he licked away every bit of the sweet nectar she provided for him.

His cock pressed hard against his boxers for he had

become hard as a brick and felt the pre-cum dripped from his tip.

He couldn't wait anymore, so he rose up and shoved his boxers down his legs like a man possessed.

"Are you ready for me, Victoria?" he asked.

She moaned, still in her euphoric afterglow.

"No, baby. I want to hear you say it. Tell me how much you want me."

"I want you, Andrei," she said. "Need you. Please."

Her words took away any restraint he had left. He guided his tip to her opening and felt the wetness that still lingered there. His cock throbbed as he pushed into her hot, dripping pussy that belonged to him. Her body was his. All of her belonged to him, and he was going to make sure she understood it now and remembered that in the future.

Victoria felt so good around him that he had to keep from coming too soon. He stilled himself, forcing his body to cooperate until they both had their fill.

When he finally regained some sense of control, he moved. Victoria sighed into his ear, and he immediately wanted more. He found a steady rhythm moving in and out of her. She held onto his shoulders as if she was holding on for dear life, but even that wasn't enough for him. He needed primal and raw ecstasy. He wanted her to claw at his back and scream his name.

Her pussy gripped his cock hard, testing his patience and endurance. If she wanted more, he could give her all she wanted and then some.

He picked up each stroke, each thrust powerful and hard so they both felt it and remembered. Thrashing around, scratching, biting one another like this was their last fuck ever. He didn't know if his desperation after his father told him to end it flavored his urgency, but it wasn't long until he felt her orgasm thrum through her body and into him, setting him off. He followed her peak and exploded deep inside of her, filling her with every essence of him.

They came together and returned back to reality before collapsing in each other's arms. There was no more doubt in his mind. This woman belonged to him. She was his, and no one was ever going to take her away from him. That was a silent oath he made to himself, and he would be damned if he'd ever break it.

CHAPTER 11

VICTORIA

"WHY AM I getting a call from a prominent judge asking you be removed from the Stavenoff case? You haven't even been back in court a day!" District Attorney Andrew Smith ran his fingers through his already graying hair. Being DA took a toll on you, no matter who you were or how well you did your job.

"I know, sir," Victoria said. She was expecting to have a little more time before she talked to her boss about what happened in court, but apparently Judge Hughes moved fast. She'd come clean to her boss about her and Andrei. There was no other choice, and she wasn't a liar, despite the reputation lawyers made for themselves. "I am still able to do my job well, sir. I didn't mean for this to happen. I promise."

"Well, I hope not. This isn't some nightly television drama, Bellamy. We practice real law here. More than that, we're public servants who represent the people. Most public legal systems would let you go even at the hint of a scandal."

"We didn't know we'd be facing each other in court again." The room was spinning, and she felt nauseous. Recently, she wasn't handling stress well.

"Even associating with Mr. Rusak after that first case was bad enough. It doesn't matter that you weren't on opposing sides during the start of your... relationship. What matters is that the press and the public will see the worst. Maybe even think you two manipulated the case."

"Sir, you know me. I would never—"

"Bellamy, I know that. The public doesn't."

She understood what he was saying. It didn't matter that she and Andrei weren't lovers during the first case. That was one of the bad parts about being a state prosecutor. People always thought the worst. You were guilty until proven otherwise.

Smith sighed and sat back in his chair. He tossed a folder over to her.

"What's this, sir?"

"Read it."

She pulled the papers out and was stunned by what she read. "A recommendation letter?"

"Not just any recommendation letter. Chicago is looking for a new DA, and I told them you'd be perfect for the job."

"Me? District Attorney?"

"Don't seem so surprised, Bellamy. Before your injury, you were at the top of your game. I dare say you are the best ADA I've had the honor of working with. But now..."

"I promise. It's just...I thought I had to work a few more years before I was even considered for this."

"You know me, Bellamy. I don't give my praise often, so when I do it counts. You're one of the best prosecutors in this department, which is why it'd be a shame to waste your talents by keeping you here."

"Sir—"

He held his hand out to stop her. "This is the opportunity of a lifetime, Bellamy. Any other prosecutor would jump at the chance to take it. Due to recent circumstances, I'm sure we can wait a little while before you make your decision. I want to be certain you don't take this opportunity lightly."

"No, sir. I never do that."

"Good to hear it. That will be all then, but don't take too long to think about this or it may not be here when you finally make a decision."

She stood up. "I understand, sir. Thank you."

Deedee and Roslyn were in her office when she got back.

"So? What did he say?" Deedee asked. "He didn't fire you, did he?"

"No," Victoria said. "He offered me a promotion."

"That's a good thing," Roslyn said.

"Of course that's a good thing," Deedee added.

"So why do she look like someone killed your cat?" Roslyn asked.

"He offered me a DA position," Victoria said.

Roslyn squinted her eyes. "That doesn't make any sense. He's the DA."

"Not here. He offered me the DA position in Chicago."

Deedee hugged her. "Holy shit, girl. That's amazing."

"He's offering you the chance of a lifetime," Roslyn said. "You'd be a crazy fool not to take it, so what's with the hesitation?"

Victoria tried to think of how to voice her words without sounding like a complete idiot. Roslyn was right. She would be crazy not to take up the offer, there was only one strong reason for her not to do it. She hesitated before saying anything, but somehow they knew.

"It's that lawyer you've been crushing on, isn't it?" Deedee asked.

"Any other time I would've jumped on this without thinking about it. Now, I don't know what to do."

Victoria didn't realize how strong her feelings for Andrei were until the thought of possibly leaving him sunk in. She hadn't planned for any of this to happen, but she was in deep and wasn't sure if she could ever let go. Andrei had crept in and become a part of her somehow, even if she didn't know what that part was exactly.

"Tell you what, we'll grab lunch and talk it over," Deedee said.

"I don't feel much like eating anything," Victoria said, sitting on her desk.

"My treat today, especially with so much on your mind."

Roslyn arched her brow. "So now you have money to spend?"

"What? This is helping a friend in need. I'm all about helping friends."

"Oh, I'm sure."

Victoria smiled. Her friends' lighthearted bickering

softened her mood a bit, and she finally let them drag her to a nearby café.

She wasn't hungry, but she could use some time away from the office. Besides, she could use some advice on what she should do, because she didn't trust herself to make any good decisions at the moment. She ordered a ham and turkey chef salad and a medium soft drink, but she just picked at the food in her bowl.

Her friends Roslyn and Deedee were ecstatic about her new job offer. Victoria wished she could be as excited as they were.

"So are you in love with him?" Deedee asked.

"I don't know. Isn't it too soon to be in love with him?"

"Only you can answer that one," Roslyn said.

Victoria said, "I don't want to leave him, but I don't know what to do."

"You could ask him to go with you," Rosalyn said. "If he really cares about you, you at least consider it."

"I can ask him to do that, give up his life for me."

"Isn't that what you'd be doing if you didn't go?"

"People make sacrifices for the people they care about," Deedee said. "If you love him, maybe you should stay here and work on your relationship. You can always find another job since you are a lawyer, right?"

Victoria answered, "I guess you are right about that."

Deedee said, "If this man is the love of your life, don't leave. You may end up regretting it."

"That's not fair." Roslyn took a sip of her water before continuing. "Why should she be the one to have to give up her career for him? He should at least be willing to do the same thing."

The decisions were making Victoria dizzy. "I don't feel well. Maybe I shouldn't eat this salad." She beckoned their waitress over. "Take another ginger ale, please?"

When the waitress returned, she tried to drink the fresh ginger ale, but nausea overtook her. She bolted to the bathroom, and she barely made the toilet before everything in her stomach came rushing out. She heard footsteps behind her, but she didn't dare look up for fear of getting sick again.

"You okay, girl?" Deedee asked.

"I don't know. I think so." Victoria closed her eyes, hoping to push the dizzy feeling away.

"Maybe we should take you to the doctor," Deedee said.

"Is there any chance you might be..." Roslyn's voice trailed off.

"Might be what?" Deedee asked. "Are you asking her?"

"If she could be pregnant."

That loaded word hit Victoria but the sack of bricks, and it made her lurch over the toilet again. There was no way... "Oh, hell," Victoria said. She had not used a condom when she'd been with Andrei. She been so consumed by him, so lost in the sensations he was giving her that she hadn't cared.

"So it's possible?" Roslyn asked. "You really could be pregnant?"

"Maybe," she said. "It might be too early to tell."

Deedee perked up. "You definitely need to go to the doctor. Immediately."

"Yeah," Rosalyn, said. "You should take the rest of the day off. You don't look too hot, sweetie."

"Maybe I should go home and lie down."

"Don't worry," Rosalyn said. Victoira felt her friend's hand rubbing her back, comforting her. "We'll cover for you."

"We got this," Deedee said. "I'll pick you up in the morning. My OB-GYN has walk-in hours then, and she's one of the best in the area. She loves her patients."

Victoria wasn't strong enough to argue. "All right."

"We're calling you a cab," Rosalyn said.

After she got home, she couldn't rest. What if she was pregnant? Did that mean her career was over? How was she going to tell Andrei if she was?

She tried sleeping, but it was useless. Nervousness filled her at all the things that could go wrong if she was pregnant. She couldn't find a comfortable position.

She needed to see Andrei. She needed to feel his arms around her to comfort her and make her feel that everything would be okay. She knew that she needed to see him right away.

Instead of calling, she went straight over there when she thought he'd be home, giving him enough time to travel home.

She knocked, and when he opened the door, she held on to him.

"Hey," he said, chuckling. "This is a needed surprise. I was just thinking about you."

"I thought about you too." She took in the strong and exotic scent of his cologne and allowed it to wrap around her, until she couldn't think of anything but him.

"I was just about to make dinner," he said. "Care to join me?"

She thought about food, and her stomach growled.

She didn't have anything in her stomach since she'd gotten sick earlier.

He laughed at the sound. "I'll take that as a yes. Get comfortable. I can start the stove up."

She let him take her jacket and followed him into the kitchen. There was something so peaceful about watching him cook. It was so domestic and not like her at all, but yet he was sexy as hell as he moved, which showed nothing but strength in his masculine frame as he moved from the refrigerator to the stove and to the counter.

As he cooked, she thought about the job offer in Chicago. Her friends and boss were all right. It was one of the best opportunities she'd ever had, and it could be the only one she'd ever see.

Any other time in her career, before meeting Andrei, and she would have been ecstatic with the offer. Making DA at her age was an accomplishment in itself, but as a black woman, it was even more rewarding. She'd be crazy not to accept it, because an opportunity of this caliber might never come around again.

Roslyn could have had a point earlier. She and

Andrei could move to Chicago and start a new life together. It'd be refreshing to be away from the jobs that were now in question because of their relationship.

She immediately shook that fantasy out of her head. They hadn't been together long enough to make a long-term decision like that. They hadn't even been out more than a few times together, but already she was planning their future. She had to be totally insane.

Now, she could possibly be pregnant. It was all too much to handle.

"You look like you're thinking too hard over there," Andrei said. "How about some wine?"

"Okay. I mean, no. I'm fine."

"You sure? Look like you could use something to relax." He poured a glass for himself.

She nodded, not trusting herself to speak.

"You going to tell me what's got you all freaked out? You look a little down. It isn't your office giving you hell because of me?"

"That's part of it."

"I'll come there and tell them my side. They have to know we did nothing wrong. Neither one of us would have entered that courtroom if we knew we were facing each other."

"I appreciate the offer, but you coming to my job would only make things worse. Think of how your office would react to me showing up defending you."

"I guess you have a point."

"There is something I wanted to tell you."

He took out ingredients for a salad and mixed the vegetables in a bowl, and she thought about the salad she couldn't eat earlier.

"I'm all ears. What's on your mind, baby?"

There was that word again. Even his endearments were hitting her with steady reminders of their unprotected nights together.

"My boss offered me a promotion today," she said, watching for his reaction.

"Really? That's great!" He stopped messing with

the salad and came around the counter to kiss her and pull her into his arms. "Why would you be nervous to share that with me?"

She didn't want him to pull away. When he held her, it was the only time she had a clear head and blocked everything else that was on her mind like none of it even existed.

It was now or never. She needed to know at least part of his thoughts on the craziness that was now her life.

"He offered me a DA position. It's in Chicago." He continued holding her, so she wasn't sure if he'd heard her or not.

He finally pulled away, and she wasn't sure what she read in his eyes.

"What did you say?" he asked.

Andrei was so still that she couldn't even see him breathing.

"I haven't given him an answer yet. He told me to think about it."

"What's there to think about? This is something that's big for you."

He moved away from here, and she instantly felt the distance between them increase more than just physically. It was like he had shut off a part of himself to talk to her.

"You should consider it," he said. He'd gone back to fixing the salad, but now he avoided her eyes. His voice even sounded cold and distant.

"Why would you say that?"

"Because I know how much your work means to you. I've seen you in action, Victoria. You were made to be a District Attorney."

"Everyone keeps telling me that."

"You keep hearing it because it's true."

"I thought out of everyone, you'd be the one person to talk me out of it."

"Is that what you want?"

"Maybe. I don't know what I want, Andrei. That's why I came here."

"I'd never want to be the one to hurt you, and I'm not going to be the asshole who talks you out of your dream. I know how hard you've worked for this. I would never do hold you back."

What if she wanted him to? Maybe she needed someone who wasn't so damn supportive and pulled her the other way for a change. Why couldn't he be the one to do that?

"Come with me." The words left her lips before she'd even had time to process what that meant to either of them.

"What?" At least he finally looked at her that time. "What exactly are you asking me?"

"We could both go to Chicago...together."

He ran his fingers through his hair. "Just up and leave everything?"

"I didn't mean it like that. I just thought..."

He leaned over and grabbed her hand. "I'm not upset. In any other lifetime, I'd be happy to at least consider going with you, but I can't leave New York."

"I get it. Your family's practice needs you. It'd be ridiculous for them to just let you move like that."

"It's not about my father's law firm. I wish it were that simple."

Her anxiety raced back as she tried to decipher his meaning. "I know we've barely been together long enough to make that kind of decision."

"That's not it either. Victoria, I have no doubt about us. That's not what I'm saying."

"Then just tell me. I'm a big girl, Andrei. I can take it." When he didn't say anything, she brought up one of the reason's she worried about in the back of her mind but never voiced out loud. "Is it because I'm black and you're white?"

She jumped when he dropped the salad for and it clanged to the ground. He was on her side of the counter before she even knew what was happening.

Andrei gripped her shoulders tightly and kissed her like a man possessed. It wasn't gentle or soft. His lips and tongue invaded hers until thoughts weren't even there to haunt her mind anymore. He consumed her, and she had no choice but to do the same to him.

When he pulled back, his face was filled with determination and some anger, but it didn't feel directed at her.

"Don't you ever think I don't want you because of something as stupid as that," he said. "Ever."

She smiled as he kissed her again, and she tried to do as he demanded and push all thoughts of that out of her head for good. She already had too much to going on in there, and she'd find out soon enough if she had something else of his to worry about.

CHAPTER 12

ANDREI

WHEN VICTORIA SAID THOSE WORDS, he'd nearly lost it. That'd she'd even think it made him want to kiss that shit away and replace it with something more real: how much he wanted her. Erik was right. Nothing like that mattered.

Andrei had developed some strong feelings for Victoria, and it blew his mind just how much he cared about her. Was it love?

He'd been in love before, but it was nothing like this. His past relationships had been hard and draining. Being with Victoria felt easy and real.

If he wanted something more with her, he had to get past his damn stubbornness and come clean to her. He needed to tell her about the two people in his life who were his world. It wasn't going to get easier. He also knew the longer he put it off, the more excuses he'd make for not saying anything. That would only make her angry with him, and her anger would break him.

"Victoria, I have something important to talk to you about." He took her hand and led her to the couch. Dinner would have to wait, because his news couldn't.

"Is it something bad?" she asked.

How did he answer that? To him, Asya and Nadia were the two best things he'd ever done, even if their mother made it difficult for him. "That depends on how you look at it. To me, it isn't." He sat down and pulled her close to him on the couch. He needed to touch her, in case it was one of the last times she'd let him. "There's a reason why I can't leave any time soon."

"You're making me nervous," she said and gripped his hand tight. "Just tell me you aren't secretly married or something."

He couldn't help letting out a chuckle, which

relieved some of his tension. "I'm not married. I was, but we got a divorce."

"Oh," she said. "Good." She swallowed hard, obviously waiting for the other shoe to drop.

He took a deep breath. "While we were married, we had two kids."

Her eyes widened. "Kids?"

Andrei never took his eyes off of her as he spoke. "Two girls, actually. Asya, who's seven, and Nadia, who's ten."

She stood up, disconnecting the warmth he'd depended on. "Kids? Two girls? You're just telling me this now?"

"I wanted so badly to tell you."

"Why didn't you, Andrei? One kid is a pretty big deal, but you have two!" She paced back and forth in front of him.

"It never seemed like the right time. Everything between us has happened so fast."

"I'm sure there was some time in there when you could've mentioned fathering children."

He stood and took her hands, and he was grateful that she didn't pull away. "That's why I'm telling you now. I didn't want this to go any farther until I told you."

"So they don't live with you?" she asked.

Her voice was calm, and he couldn't read what she was thinking, so he answered the best he could.

"No. My ex-wife has primary custody. It wasn't an easy relationship. We got together when we were young and stupid. We didn't really split on good terms, so she took it out on me by keeping the kids. That's why I can't just go with you. If I leave town, I will never see them. She's vindictive enough to make sure that never happens, and she's been that way ever since the divorce six years ago."

"I knew you were divorced. I found that out when I researched you before we met, but it said nothing about you having kids."

"I protect them from anything related to my job. I do my best to make sure no one goes near them or has access to them. In case..."

"In case you actually defend the bad guys?"

He nodded since he couldn't tell her the type of people he had to defend in the past. Bad was putting it lightly. His father had worked with some of the most ruthless bastards in the city. Some that weren't exactly easy to work for without a guarantee they'd get off and who weren't against using information about his children in case Andrei failed to win.

The risk to his family was one of the main reasons why he and his father bickered so much. Andrei wanted to deal with the people who weren't a threat to his family. His father's theory was that the worst ones had the deepest pockets, and if Rusak & Associates did their job the way they'd always done, they'd never lose a court case.

Andrei refused to risk it. That's why he dealt with the ones who were being charged with less heinous crimes. Most of the suspects he represented were just stupid enough to get caught but not smart enough to consider ransoming their lawyer's kids. Andrei would die before letting any of his clients use his children for leverage, even the so-called innocent ones.

"This is a lot to take in," she said, sitting back

down. "I don't really know what to say to you. Hiding something like this... I have been nothing but straightforward with you since the beginning. Now you're telling me you have children."

"The last thing I ever wanted to do was hurt you, and I couldn't stand it if you hated me for this."

"I don't hate you, but I'm upset. I think that's reasonable."

She sat so still that he knew she was still in shock. He'd probably be too if their roles were reversed. Knowing how he inherited his father's quick temper, he probably wouldn't be taking it as well as she was.

"Of course it is. I'm so sorry, Victoria."

"I just wish you didn't wait so long to tell me. It's all just overwhelming, especially now."

"Because of your promotion?" he asked.

"Yes," she said. "That and there's a lot going on that I have to deal with."

He could tell she was holding something back in her answer, but he couldn't push her to say any more. Not when he wasn't sure how she was taking all of it.

"You don't have to deal with any of this alone. I meant what I said. I want us to figure this thing out together. Don't you?"

"I don't know. I thought I wanted to find out what's between us, but I'm just so confused."

"Please don't let this hold us back from doing that, from still discovering what we have."

"I'm not the one keeping us from moving forward. You're the one who waited to spill this out. Why now? Why tell me this tonight?"

"Because I want more than just sex with you. I care about you, and I want all of you, but I can't demand that until you know what being with me involves."

"You want all of me?" she asked, her voice going a little high, as if doubting his words.

"I want everything from you," he said. He needed to touch her, feel her skin against his. His body craved that more than the air that he needed to breathe. He stood and inched closer to her. When she didn't move, he pulled her tense body to his so he could kiss the side of her face. He whispered against her. "Baby, I'm so sorry. Can you forgive me? I know I should have told you. I promise to be nothing but honest with you from now on. I promise."

She tensed up a little and then moved out of his reach again.

With each time she did that it was like she pulled a part of him with her. It killed him to see her act like she didn't love him.

"No, Andrei. This is too big for you to just try to make me forget with a damn kiss. You have kids. Children I never knew about. I can't believe I asked you to go with me to Chicago. What was I thinking?"

"I'm honored that you'd even ask that. Don't you ever regret that."

"I know better than this, but I got sucked in. Ever since Montego Bay, I've been consumed with this relationship, with you."

"And that's a bad thing?"

"It is when I don't know who I am when I'm with you. I forget the real world, Andrei, and that's not a good thing. Not for people like me who have to protect the people in that reality. The world still exists outside those doors, and you've made that clear tonight."

"Calm down, Victoria."

"Don't do that. Don't tell me to calm down. This isn't a calm-down moment. It's a freak-the-fuck-out moment. I just don't think I have the energy to be as angry as I should."

"Good. I don't want you angry."

"Of course you don't. You want me to just accept it as if it's nothing and be the good, understanding one in all of this."

"I didn't say that."

"The idea of being a parent scares me."

"You don't have to worry about that anytime soon. I don't want you to think I'm out looking for a second mother for them. That's not why I'm with you." He tried to take her hand, but she moved away again. He sat in a seat to give her the space she wanted. "I care about you so much."

"Then why lie to me?"

"I didn't set out to lie to you. I just didn't tell you. There's a difference."

"Not telling me something that big is like lying. Don't act like a lawyer with me. This isn't a courtroom."

"It's starting to feel like one."

"What's that supposed to mean?"

"It's just that we can talk about this like two adults and figure it out together without it turning into you versus me. There's no winner and loser here. Sit down, and we can figure it out. I'm sure we can." He gestured to the matching seat, which gave some space between them unlike the couch had. He hated not being closer to her, but he'd give her all the distance she needed. Even though he wanted to storm over there and kiss the anger away like he'd kissed that race nonsense out of her earlier.

"I can't sit beside you right now," she said. "I'm too upset."

Their first fight and he didn't know what to say to ease her mind. He ran his fingers through his hair.

When the evening began, she'd wanted him to think about Chicago and the possibility of going there with her. Now, it felt like she wouldn't want him within a couple of inches of her. That irritated him more than he wanted it to because the woman in front of him was all he could ever hope to find in a partner. She was feisty, determined, gorgeous, and the total package. She made his cock ache without even being in the same room as him. She impacted him that much.

"Tell me what you want," Andrei said. "Tell me what you need me to do, and I'll do it." He offered and knew he'd hate giving her that choice, but if he didn't he knew she'd really grow to hate him then.

Maybe he'd been wrong about where he and Victoria were headed. He'd been wrong before. His ex-wife, Trish, had been wrong for him, but that had been a tumultuous relationship from the beginning. They fought angry and fucked angry. It wasn't a healthy relationship and certainly not one he wanted his kids to see. Seeing how scared their daughters had been after a loud fight had been one of the key factors in his decision to move forward with the divorce. They'd tried marriage counseling, but it had been ugly. Andrei had had a series of low-key one night stands since his divorce, but nothing too serious. He broke things off if he thought that they were going somewhere. He was just too busy to deal with stuff like this...like Victoria refusing to work things out.

"Maybe we should take a break from each other," she said. "This all has happened so fast. Maybe we need a few days to figure it out on our own first."

How was separating going to help them work this shit out? He didn't say it, because he wanted her to know this was her decision. Even though he fucking hated where it was leading.

"I don't want that," he said. "You have to know that's the last thing I want."

"I need it, Andrei. Give me a few days to find my head and get back into everything. Then we can talk."

"A few days. That's it." She started to protest, but he held up his hand. "A few days, like you said. You'll know by then. You have to."

"You sound so sure," she said.

"I am."

The silence between them stretched until it almost became a living thing that he could see. He wanted to chop it off with a damn axe as he waited for what she'd say next.

"All right," Victoria finally said. "Just give me a few days, and then we can talk."

He nodded even though he knew those few days were going to feel like lifetimes.

It wasn't over, no matter what decision she came to. He wasn't going to ever let Victoria Bellamy go, even if he had to storm in that fucking District Attorney's office and drag her back to his place kicking and screaming. He'd give her a few days, and if she didn't make the right decision, he was going to be there to remind her that there was only one decision to make, and he was it.

CHAPTER 13

VICTORIA

VICTORIA TRIED to get all her crying out before Deedee arrived the next morning, but she was still doing it when her friend rang her doorbell.

"Are you ready to go?" Deedee asked when she opened her door. Then she noticed her wet face. "Oh, honey." She hugged Victoria tight. "Pregnancy isn't that bad. I promise, and you may not even be pregnant."

She didn't have the energy to tell her friend that it was so much more than that. She also left out the fact that she'd gone to the nearest pharmacy and convenience store to buy three pregnancy tests.

She'd downed so much water and diet tea to pee on those damn sticks, all three of them. She was positive she wasn't the first woman to cry on the closed toilet after reading the same three results. Positive. That was a joke in itself. Positive wasn't a happy thing to celebrate when she wasn't even sure where she stood with the baby's father.

Andrei was a woman's dream: rich, confident, and sexy. He was one hell of a good lawyer, going by his track record. She could have just accepted him having kids and stayed with him, but she couldn't. What he'd done felt like betrayal in the worst way.

Her ex-boyfriend had betrayed her, too. Sure he cheated and blamed her for spending too much time on cases. It was a different type of betrayal, but what Andrei had done still hurt her.

"Let's go before I depress the hell out of both of us," she said after pushing away from the hug.

She had a lot of respect for Deedee by the time they got to the doctor's office. Her friend talked the entire time, but she didn't demand Victoria's undivided attention or response, almost as if she knew mindless chatter about nothing was needed to lessen the stress of the situation. It was refreshing to get lost in someone else's drama for twenty minutes without having to be an active participant.

Victoria signed in and filled out the necessary paperwork that was almost long enough to distract her from the reason why she was in the doctor's office in the first place. She sat and fiddled with her phone while Deedee talked her ears off and kept her company in the sterile waiting room with magazines that were probably a couple years old.

When they finally called her name, she asked for Deedee to come back with her. Yeah, she was strong enough to put on her big-girl panties and be the strong woman she was when she was a prosecutor, but she didn't want to be strong. She needed all the support and help she could get at the moment, and she could see Deedee's appreciative smile as they went to the back together.

The doctor was an OB-GYN specialist named Dr. Jacob James, and Deedee was right. He was a prominent doctor. Victoria couldn't have chosen better on her own. Considering that she normally thoroughly researched every major decision, that was saying something.

Still her trained mind had taught her not to trust too easily. Victoria had prosecuted enough idiots to make that a personal rule, but she'd also had problems trusting most people. That's why Andrei surprised her. She'd trusted him easily, which wasn't like her at all.

The nurse came in and took Victoria across the hall, where she had her blood drawn, provided them a urine sample, and got on the dreaded scale to get her weight, which was already higher than she thought it was. Already she wanted to go home and crawl back into bed, but she forced herself to stay put. She'd never run from anything in her life, and she wasn't running from this.

"Ms. Bellamy," the nurse said, "I'm going to need you to undress and put on this gown. Then sit back on the examination table."

Deedee gave her a moment to change, standing with her back to Victoria and looking at some sort of horrifying diagram that explained the parts of the uterus. That gave her a minute to collect herself before she wound up having a crying fit in front of the doctor.

She hated doctors' offices and any kind of medical facility. They felt so sterile and void of life, plus they smelled weird. Then she realized court was similar in a way. Waiting in one room for a person to tell you the outcome of your life was never fun.

"Ready to go. You don't have to look at that poster anymore."

After Deedee turned around, Dr. James and the nurse soon came in.

"Good Morning, Mrs. Bellamy. I'm Dr. James and this is Nurse Pratchett."

She sighed as she shook his hand. "It's Ms. Bellamy. I'm not married." He seemed a little shocked by that, but he didn't say anything. If he did, she couldn't promise not to knock him on his butt. She was in that kind of mood today.

Dr. James turned to his nurse and asked, "Could you help Ms. Bellamy get on the table and into the stirrups please?"

Victoria shuffled around as the nurse helped her climb into the awkward position on the exam table. "Oh, Lord," she thought. "Let the home tests be a mistake. I can't be pregnant. Not now. What would I do with a baby on my own? I'd scar the baby for life. I just know it. I can't even have a normal romantic relationship, and now I'm going to be a mother."

The nurse assisted her to position to the most comfortable position she could be in with her legs up in the stirrups and open wide in a cold and sterile room.

The doctor examined her cervix, palpated and measured her abdomen, and listened to her heart. Victoria felt like a prize pig who was being looked over thoroughly.

"We have a quick-result method of testing for pregnancy hormones. The results of your blood test came back positive," Dr. James said. "Congratulations. You're going to be a mother."

Deedee clapped her hands together. "I knew it. That's so exciting."

Victoria wished she could be excited like her friend.

"According to your chart and last period, you're not that far along. Probably three weeks or so at most."

"You can tell this early?" she asked.

"Well, with blood tests and calculations of your last cycle, we can pretty much chart the time. We can't see the baby through ultrasound just yet because it's so small, but I'd like you to come back in a couple of weeks so we can see how you're coming along."

"This is insane." The room felt like it was caving in on her. She put her head on her forehead. "I don't feel well."

"What are you experiencing?"

"Dizziness and I'm tired all the time."

"That's certainly normal," the doctor said. "Your body is adjusting to providing nutrients to prepare for the baby. I'm going to prescribe you some neonatal vitamins along with iron, which should both help restore some of your energy and balance you out. I want you to take one of each every day until I see you in a couple of weeks."

"I'm not a fan of pills," she said. She hated taking any kind of medication or vitamins regularly.

"These are mild, and the pills will help. You may want to take it easy for a couple of days until your energy returns."

"I already took time off for my ankle. I can't take off anymore."

"Work should be fine," he said. "Just avoid too much strenuous activity until you feel yourself again. Sit down as much as you can."

That was the problem. She was pregnant. There was no feeling-like-herself place to ever go back to. Not only that. Now she had to worry about telling Andrei when she was hoping to avoid him for as long as she could. She still had to process his bombshell.

What would he think? He already had two kids, and they hadn't even been together long enough to discuss it. She didn't even know if he'd be a good father.

She'd really done it this time. Andrei had changed her whole life in the space of a few weeks. It wasn't all his fault. She was a grown woman, and she didn't stop him from doing anything. In fact, she wanted him to. Over and over again.

It annoyed her that even then she could feel her body craving him, longing for his touch. The way he kissed her and made her call out for him...she just couldn't forget about him.

"Ms. Bellamy, are you listening?" Dr. James said.

"I'm sorry," she said pushing all sexual thoughts of Andrei to the back of her mind, but she knew they'd be back before long.

"Don't forget to schedule your appointment with the receptionist. l want you to come back in two weeks for a checkup and ultrasound, but be sure to contact my office if your dizziness or fatigue increases."

"Okay," Victoria said, dreading coming back. She hated her yearly physical and going to the dentist. Now, she had another medical professional to add to her list.

"It was a pleasure meeting you," he said.

"Thank you, doctor."

He stopped to chat with Deedee briefly about her kids before leaving them.

"Do you want me to go and make your appointment, while you get dressed?" Deedee asked.

"You're a godsend, Deedee," Victoria said. "I'd appreciate it. The faster we get out of here, the better I'll feel."

"You didn't like Dr. James? I thought he was great."

"It's not that. I'm just not a fan of doctors' offices."

"Got you. Don't worry. We'll be out of here before you know it."

She told her friend the days that were good for her and Deedee left her to make the appointment. Victoria wondered what her boss would think. The promotion didn't seem possible now. Maybe he'd let her pass on the offer and stay in New York. They didn't seem like too much to ask. She always looked up to him and respected him. That had to count for something, right?

Victoria and Deedee left the doctor's office together.

Deedee talked as they walked out to hail a cab. "I thought you were pregnant when you started vomiting. That's one of the first signs."

"I don't know what I'm going to do next. I've never even considered what I would do if I had a kid. How do you even manage it?"

"Day by day," Deedee said. "I am taking you home so you can get some rest."

"What? No. There's no way I'm missing another day of work."

"Smith will understand. He is a lawyer, and you're pregnant. He has to understand. I'm pretty sure there's a law against him not understanding."

As much as Deedee protested, Victoria didn't change her mind. She went to work like she always did, and being pregnant wasn't going to keep her from doing it.

When she got to the office, she wasted no time going straight to DA Smith's office. She wasn't taking any chances on him finding out from someone else. As much as she trusted Deedee and Rosalyn, the rest of the office were natural-born gossipers. If they had a bone, they would run with it, and the last thing she needed was another scandal.

Smith was on the phone when she entered his open office, but he beckoned her to sit down. She closed the door before doing so, because she didn't want a nosy intern to pass by while there is talking.

"Heck, figure it out!" Smith slammed the telephone down on the receiver. "What is it, Bellamy?"

"I can come back later, sir," she said. This was certainly not a good time, and she didn't want to talk to him when he was in a bad mood.

"You're here. Just say what you came to tell me."

She gripped her hands together tightly. "About the position."

"Yeah? What about it?"

"I was wondering if there's any possible way to accept the DA position and do the work from here." She didn't think that there was a way to make it happen, but she might as well ask.

He looked at her the same way he stared at new employees to see if he could get under their skin and make them squirm.

Even though she was nervous, she wasn't going to back down from looking at him. She stared down many bad men in the courtroom. Her boss wasn't going to send her running.

"Let me get this straight. You want the position, but instead of going to Chicago, where the job is, you will do the work from here?"

"When you put it like that, the whole thing sounds ridiculous."

"That's because it is ridiculous, Bellamy! I recommend you for one of the most prestigious job positions a state can offer an attorney, and you return to say you want to have your cake and eat it too? You can't have it both ways. Either accept the job and go to Chicago, or turn it down and stay here. There is no other option."

"Under different circumstances, sir, I wouldn't even think of asking you this. But this morning, I got news that's going to change everything for me."

"Don't tell me someone died. I just got off the phone with one of my other attorneys. There's only so much death a man can take it one day."

"No one died. I'm just... pregnant."

He smiled. "Is this fuck with the boss day? Tell me this is a joke."

"I wish it was, sir. I really do."

"Bellamy, I took a big risk recommending you for that position. There were even a couple of people who are more qualified than you, but they don't have your tenacity and bravado when it comes to getting shit done. Anyone in this office has the potential to do some good in this damn world, it's you. Now, you come and tell me that you can't accept the position because you're pregnant?"

"I know what you're thinking."

"No. I'm positive you don't know what I'm thinking. You may feel that I'm mad at you, but I'm not. If anything, I'm disappointed. I don't have any children, you know that. This job has been my wife and my child for years. Some can do it with the family and others can't. Even the ones with the family can never commit as much as those without. Just the way it is. There's no harm in it." He leaned forward, and a form of sincerity filled his eyes that she never got to see often. "But I thought you are like me, vicious in the courtroom because you know the bad people who'd be roaming around out there hurting other people if it weren't for us. We're the ones who come early and stay late, not because we have to, but because we want to. Without that kind of dedication, who knows what the justice system would be like?"

She didn't know what to say. Earlier in her career, that was exactly what she was like. It's why she left the private firm in the first place. No amount of money was enough to make up for the feeling she got when she put a known criminal behind bars.

The pay was shitty and the hours were long, but she got a rush every time she saw how happy people were when they saw that justice had finally prevailed. In a world where that wasn't often, she savored the times when it happened. She knew Smith felt the same way. It was a drive neither one of them could describe to someone who hadn't been through it, who hadn't lived it. That's what made her job one of the most rewarding parts of living. She never wanted to throw that away, even if she was pregnant. But she had to adjust her life accordingly, that was obvious.

She almost preferred seeing her boss' anger rather than his regret, because she knew what he was saying. As much as she would try to do everything in her power to be the same way she was before getting pregnant, there was no way it could ever be the same. Many people accepted that, but she knew that part of her would always wonder how far she could've gone and how great she could've been at her job as the DA of Chicago.

"I'm sorry," she said.

"No more than I am," he said.

Although she knew he didn't mean to hurt her that way, it still felt like a knife being shoved in her gut and yanked back out. She nodded and left his office without saying anything else. She wrote to her office as quickly as she could and shut the door. She didn't want anyone to see how heartbroken she was or the tears that started falling from her eyes again.

"DIDN'T I tell you this would happen?"

Andrei wasn't a day drinker, but he'd stopped by Erik's bar for a drink. He needed one. Plus he wanted his father off his ass. He didn't need that shit today. Not now.

"I doubt you foresaw this exactly," Andrei said.

"But I told you she was going to get upset about your daughters. You can't just keep something that big a secret."

"Wasn't trying to lie to her. I just wanted to enjoy being with her before something like that got in the way. And look what happened, no Victoria."

"You brought this on yourself, man. No one else to

blame about it, and that whiskey isn't going to help you much either."

"Probably not, but it sure feels like it could numb the way that I'm feeling right now."

"What's up with heartbroken people wanting to feel numb? How the hell does that help anything? If it was me, I want to feel every damn stab. Even if it killed me. That's what life's about, feeling it."

Andrei groaned. "No philosophy today. I can't take it right now."

"I thought you lawyers were all about philosophy, which is all about discovering truth. Just so you know."

Andrei drained his glass and shook the ice cubes to get his friend to notice.

"No more for you. Cutting you off."

"I'm not drunk yet. I need at least another two to get there."

"Have you heard? Day drinking is bad for you."

"It's a stigma. No one ever said it's bad for you.

Right now, I'll take whatever I can get. That makes you my friend, my bartender, and my priest."

"You're not Catholic."

"It's a new day, and I can be whatever I want to be. Drunk, Catholic, it doesn't matter."

"You sure you aren't drunk? You sound like the idiots I have to keep reminding that last call is it."

"Not drunk. If I was, I wouldn't be thinking about her as much as I am now."

"Don't you think you should just try to talk to her?"

"She asked for space, so I'm giving her space."

"It's only been one day. At this rate, your liver may give out before you do."

Andrei was puzzled that Erik had strongly encouraged his relationship with Victoria to begin with. If he was being honest with himself, he had hoped that Erik would have talked him out of it. Not because Victoria was black but because she was another lawyer.

He heard the horror stories of other lawyers tried to have relationships with each other. Some were good enough to pursue and then they ended in a peaceful breakup. Others led to fighting during courtroom cases. A few people had even gotten fired for it due to the ethical agreements it violated at the firms they worked for, not to mention the bar association's ethics board. His place didn't have a clause like that, but his father was strict enough to punish him anyway. One mention to the bar association, and he might be banned for life.

He had a lot of time to think after Victoria left his apartment. Moving to Chicago sounded amazing, and she was someone he could see making a lifelong change like that with. New York came with baggage, the commitments he had made to his family, his father, and the father that he needed to be for his children. He needed to remain in town for them. He loved too much and needed to always be in their lives. They meant the world to him, and if he moved away, he could miss out on some important aspect of their life. Trish wouldn't give two shits about what he missed, so he had to stay to make sure they knew how much he loved them and that his ex-wife never poisoned them against him.

Out of all of his obligations, his girls were the only bright side to his life, at least until he met Victoria.

She was woman enough to handle him and then some.

Erik was right. He should have known better than to keep a secret from her. Even if he hadn't told her, she would've found out on her own. She was a smart and talented lawyer, and he never had any intention of hurting her.

"As your friend," Erik started, "you're not going to be in good shape if you wait for her to figure shit out, so your best bet is to call her before she decides to leave your ass altogether. Trust me. Sometimes you have be the one to put yourself out there first."

"Maybe," Andrei said.

"Have I ever steered you wrong?" Erik raised his eyebrows.

"Not yet, but there's always tomorrow." Andrei grinned as he threw some money down on the counter and stood up.

"You're lucky I like you or I'd be throwing your ass out of here like all the other troublemakers."

"You could, but then I turn right around and sue your ass right back just for kicks."

"Where are you going?"

"You're the one who said to contact her, so that's what I'm going to do."

"That's my boy."

Andrei shook his head as he left the bar. It looked like it was going to rain soon, so he need to figure out where he was heading. There was no way he was going back to the office. Instead, he headed toward the corner, so he could hail a cab home.

That's when he saw Victoria. She exited a building with another woman, but it wasn't the DA's office. Why wasn't she at work?

"Victoria!" He called after her, but she didn't hear. By the time he made his way to the other side of the street, they had gotten in the cab and taken off.

He turned around spotted the name of the office: Dr. Jacob James, M.D, OB-GYN.

Stood in front of the office, frozen. He couldn't move at all. What the hell was she doing there during work hours?

All kinds of possibilities went through Andrei's

had. Maybe she was there for her regular check-up. She could've needed to refill a prescription for something like birth control. A million reasons for her to be visiting that type of doctor flew through his mind, but none of the possibilities calmed him down.

There was one possibility that he wasn't sure he wanted to think about.

Thunder roared above him just before rain started to fall down. Even as he got soaked, he couldn't force himself to move away from the building.

She couldn't be. Then he remembered all the times they had been together. Passionate and scorching. Also unprotected.

He finally forced his seat to walk and stopped the first cab.

Andrei tried calling her phone, but the call went straight to voicemail. She must've turned her phone off. He gave to the cab driver directions to her building.

He almost forgot to pay the cab driver, since he was in such a rush to see her. He was close to going in, and he'd even gotten his hand on the door. Then he realized he was soaked to the bone and disheveled like a madman. He couldn't go in like that, not at her place of work and embarrass her.

There was no way he could have her angry at him again, so he stopped himself from making a fool out of him and her. Maybe two drinks were too much for the daytime.

Andrei went home and took a cold shower to wake his ass up and regain focus. He would've gone for a run if the weather had been good and not a rainy hell.

If she had gone to that doctor for the reason he suspected, he needed a clear head to confront her about it. Thoughts still hit him like punches. He felt like a punch-drunk boxer.

Waiting was another form of torture that he never got used to. Even though his experience as a lawyer had forced him to be a patient man, he wasn't very patient and couldn't see that ever changing.

When the clock struck five, he tried her phone again, hoping should pick up this time. His hope shattered, and this time it was his turn to be upset.

If she was pregnant, wouldn't she have called him by now? Hell, she should've told him she was going to see the doctor in the first place. He would've been there to support her just like any real man should. It didn't matter that being a father again scared him to death. If Victoria was pregnant, he was going to be there for his child and for her.

Fuck waiting. He was going over there, and he was going to camp outside her door until she answered.

He got out of the taxi five blocks before her building so he could walk off the pent up energy that coursed through his veins. He hit the buzzer on her door and waited. When he didn't hear any movement inside, he used his fist to bang on her door. He banged nonstop, until he heard her voice from the other side.

"All right. I'm coming, I'm coming." She opened the door before she realized who he was. "No," she said. "I can't see you right now."

She tried to close the door, but he put his foot to stop it from shutting. "We need to talk, and we need to talk now." He opened the door and pushed through.

"I did not invite you in. You can leave."

"Why did you go to see Dr. Jacob James today?"

She looked at him for a minute. "How did you know that?"

"I saw you come out of his office earlier."

"What the...were you following me? I told you I needed space, Andrei. That doesn't give you the right to go all stalker-crazy on me."

"First, you don't get to avoid the question. I saw you because that doctor's office is on the same street as my friend's bar. I saw you when I came out."

"Bar? Are you drunk?"

"Enough with acting like a prosecutor, Victoria. Answer the damn question!"

She crossed her arms, and she looked pissed. Gorgeous as all hell, but her face was full of the fury of a woman who wasn't in the mood to be played with. "You need to take that tone way down before I even consider answering you." Her eyes were spitting fire at him.

He couldn't help the hard-on that pressed against his pants, seeing her so beautiful and angry. A deep urge to kiss her rushed him, but he knew she'd only push him away or slap him if he tried. His woman was definitely working him up, but a part of him liked seeing the emotion pouring off of her. It wasn't like the fighting he had with his ex that only fueled his annoyance. Victoria had a way of making him want her while he was still angry, and that made the anger dissipate. How could this woman make him so frustrated and still make him crave her? His woman. He'd already saw her as his, and whether she knew it or not, she was going to be his. He'd already lost himself to her, even if she wanted to keep their baby a secret.

"I'm sorry," he said. "I don't want to be angry with you. It's just after seeing you leave there and not being able to call you, it has me riled up."

She sighed. "My phone died on me, and I left my charger here. I wasn't trying to block your calls. I didn't even know you tried to contact me. Even though we said you'd give me a few days, I would've answered if my phone hadn't died."

"I think seeing you going to that doctor makes the

scheduled break fly out the damn window. You're not getting space right now. Why didn't you call me right after?"

"I told you my phone was dead."

"I'm sure you could have used your friend's phone or one at the office."

"This isn't really something you want to discuss on the phone."

He moved closer to her. "Are you going to tell me why you went there or not?"

"I'm trying to figure out if you've redeemed yourself enough to know."

"Please." Andrei came to the closest to begging that he'd ever gotten in his life. Even when Trish had made her case for primary custody of their girls, he hadn't begged like this. "Just tell me. Are you pregnant?"

She nodded before finally saying, "Yes. I'm pregnant."

He sat in one of her chairs to let all of it sink in. Before he speculated, but now that he knew it was real and right there in front of him. Too many thoughts passed through hi smind. Was he ready for another kid? His family hadn't even met Victoria yet. Then there was the shock factor after they met her. Although his family was mostly made up of accepting people, he'd never brought a woman home to meet them after he'd divorced Trish, especially not one carrying his baby.

"Can you please say something? Silence is never good when you're in the room with a lawyer."

Andrei looked up at her, but he remained silent. He could see the lines of nervousness etched in her face, and he didn't like that look on her one bit. She was beautiful, and he hated that he was the source of worry. She had the flawless face of a woman that he was falling in love with. No, that wasn't right. He'd already fallen.

He was hers, and he felt it with every inch of his being. Now, she was going to have his baby. His and hers.

He stood up and walked up to her. "We are going to have a baby!" This time he didn't care if she slapped him or not. He had to kiss her and reassure her that he would accept this baby. He was still stunned, but this was a baby that was made from the most passionate moments of his life. The baby was truly a child conceived in pure love. He could never regret something like that.

She seemed taken aback by his reaction. "You're happy."

"As long as you don't make me leave again. I hated being away from you." He touched her cheek with a single finger.

A laugh finally took away the seriousness that had stayed on her face since he arrived. "It's been less than a day."

He pulled her closer to him, loving the way she fit in his arms so perfectly. He smelled her clean scent. "Still too long. I never want to be away from you or our baby." He didn't say so, but the idea of spending the rest of his life with her was quickly growing on him.

"You know you're crazy, right?"

"I know you're starting to love my crazy. Admit it.

A sporadic trip to Montego Bay, and now we're here."

"Is that all you are going to say? We need to discuss this, all of it, like responsible adults."

Andrei said, "Probably. I have to think about what's best for you, the baby, and me. I'll come to a decision about it soon."

"Excuse me, but who's carrying this baby, Rusak?"

He grinned. He kind of like how she used his last name when she needed to make a point. Damn fine lawyer in and out of the courtroom. "That would be you, Bellamy."

"Exactly. This isn't a dictatorship. If anything, it's a partnership."

"Yes, ma'am." He nuzzled her neck. "Does this mean I'm forgiven for all of my crimes and transgressions?"

"You're going to have to put in a lot of service hours before we can even mention forgiveness," Victoria said as she kissed him on the cheek.

He groaned, feeling his cock hardening more for

her. God, he needed her or he was going to lose it. "I like being of service to my public servant."

"That's a start," she giggled as he grabbed the tip of her ear with his sharp teeth. "But if this is going to work..."

"No more serious talk tonight, please," he said. "I need you, Victoria." He pressed himself into her to hit home his point. "Need you so bad. Let me take you to bed."

"But I haven't eaten anything."

"It's not food I'm craving right now. If you let me eat you, I promise to feed you and my little one well later." He was relieved when she let him pull her up and lead her to the bedroom, and he was going to keep her there until morning unless they ate a midnight snack in the kitchen.

Andrei scooped her up and carried her to her bedroom. In the span of a few weeks, this woman had captured both his heart and soul. As much as he wanted to rip her clothes off and claim her like a hungry and needy beast, he needed to show her he cared for her and loved her.

He undressed her slowly, loosening her blouse one button at a time. When he slid the shirt off, he found her crimson silk bra there to greet him with her mind-blowing offered up to him.

He was definitely a visual creature, and her tempting body only made his cock harder. He ached to be inside of her. He lost himself in her and pulled her into a kiss so he could devour her flavors. There was no way he'd ever be able to keep his hands off her. He unclasped her bra and eased it down far enough for his hands to finally cup her full breasts. They felt exactly like he remembered. She was made perfectly for him and for him alone. Victoria was his.

He'd had been fantasizing about her since they had taken a break. The sexy fantasies mixed with his moments of regret, until he didn't know which one would win. Each moment with her was like an explosion. A wild quickie with no foreplay wouldn't be enough tonight, but he saved that away on his to-do list for another time.

Andrei undid her pants as she lay back, and he slid it down to reveal crimson underwear that matched her bra.

"Such beautiful undies for me to take off you," he said. "How can one man be so lucky?"

Her laughter was so sweet and filled the room. "That's not even my fancy stuff," she said as his hand trailed over the softness of her stomach.

"Don't tease me, baby. There's only so much I can take when you look this good."

"Well, I had to wear a decent set of lingerie to the doctor. Don't want him thinking I'm a mismatched woman with no taste."

The idea of the doctor seeing her naked body filled him with jealousy. He wanted no other man to see her body. He didn't care if the man had a medical degree. He had one cock too many for Andrei's liking. He made a mental note to look up female gynecologists.

Right now, though, it didn't matter. He was going to remind Victoria what he could do and to whom that sweet heat of hers really belonged.

She was soaking wet, dripping a little, and the evidence of it was right there for him to enjoy. He touched her covered pussy and watched as she pushed her hips against his hand.

Andrei ignored his own excitement and the fullness that begged to be released. He needed a slow seduction to fulfill his needs.

"Tell me what you want," he demanded. He knew she was strong enough to ask for what she wanted. It was hot to listen to her describe what she wanted.

"I want you," she sighed.

"No, sexy. I need you to tell me specifics. Where and how." He slid her panties over and sunk a finger in her wetness, but he stopped right there. She tried to move around him and pull his finger in deeper, but he was having none of it. "You were saying?"

She moaned without saying anything at first, but then he added a second finger, still not moving his fingers much.

"Need you inside me." She ground back into the bed.

"What do you want inside of you?"

"Your fingers moving. Now!"

She was demanding, and he loved her that way. "All you have to do is tell me, and I'm happy to do it." He moved his fingers back and forth inside her slick channel until he had her grinding on his fingers. He curved them slightly to find that sweet spot of hers and moved back and forth to get her going.

"Andrei," she cried.

"Ask," he demanded.

"Your mouth."

"That sounds interesting. What do you want my mouth to do?" He could get in the habit of teasing her. There was something about her being sexually frustrated and needing him for release that made his cock harder. He loved looking at her like this, sweaty and panting...ready for him to pleasure her.

"Make me come with your mouth. Please."

He grinned with satisfaction. "My pleasure." He slipped her panties off in one smooth motion and was back inside her. She was warm and ready for him. The perfect appetizer for him to sample.

Andrei moved his fingers with greater pace as her slickness increased and brought her closer to him. His tongue dipped down to lick her and sucked on clit. He lapped at her as if he'd never get the chance to taste her sweetness again.

Her pleasure rested on him, and that power was something he could get high from. He was there to hold her as the wave of pleasure rocked her body and flushed her delicious skin. She shook in the aftermath of her orgasm, and he trailed kisses up her body. Her nipples were hard, protruding temptations for him to suckle. He quickly latched his tongue and lips to her nipples and forced more pleasure from her.

Soon those breasts would swell and grow with milk for his child, the child he'd placed deep within her. He didn't know why that only got him more excited to take her, but he had to have her now or he wasn't going to get the chance to feel her around him before he exploded.

He ached for to plunge deep inside her. Even she showed him he was taking too long to fuck her, so she wrapped her legs around his waist, pulling him close.

Andrei didn't let either one of them wait any longer. He didn't bother pushing his boxer briefs down all the way. He released his cock and found her entrance. As much as he wanted to tease her again, he saved that for another session, because he would get multiple chances to explore her voluptuous body.

They both sighed as he pushed forward and she welcomed him like a lover greeting a long-gone sailor. He took his time pushing forward and pulling back from her depths. The woman consumed every part of him, and he needed her to be engulfed by him the same way.

He groaned as he held back the pleasure trying to force him to end quickly, his eyes shut tight. He felt like he wasn't in control. With each stroke it became harder to keep from exploding inside of her. He needed to take his time to feel every part of her and allow her arms to pull him even closer.

Her moans and pants urged him forward with each stroke back. This was what he needed more than anything in the world. Feeling her tremble around him while taking him in deeper.

When the peak finally smacked into him, he made sure he brought her with him. He came hard and long, marking her inside and out with all that was him, reminding both of them that there was no one else who could compare. They were the only people who existed in the entire world as they slammed into their orgasm hard enough to last long after both of them stopped moving.

CHAPTER 15

VICTORIA

WHEN VICTORIA WENT WORK the next day, she was still sore between her legs from her night with Andrei. That man had a point to prove, and he'd done it repeatedly.

She worked on her current cases, but she still needed to figure out how to talk to her boss again. She hadn't downright denied the job offer, but she hadn't accepted either. She hoped that he hadn't called them already to tell them that she was pregnant and unable to move to Chicago. The DA position was still an option.

Although things between her and Andrei were finally at a manageable point, they still needed to talk about what a baby meant for them. What if she did decide to accept the position? Although Smith was disappointed that she was going to have a family, that didn't mean she couldn't do a damn good job, even when she had to take care of a Munchkin. She put a hand on her stomach.

Her computer had a desktop notification that she got an email from him; she was a little afraid to open it. Fear wasn't a common feeling for Victoria, and it was definitely not one she liked. In the back of her mind, she wondered if he'd ever talk to her again. Some of the staff he only talked to with one word demands. She wasn't one of them, but maybe he would after she didn't meet his expectations.

Victoria took a deep breath and opened the email.

It was a simple sentence: "The job is still yours if you want it." He'd signed it even though most people in the office didn't bother putting their name at the bottom of emails anymore.

So he hadn't given up on her completely, which made her want to cry again. She knew it was the hormones, because she wasn't the crying type. Lately, that was drastically changing. She sent up a small prayer that she wasn't going to be one of those pregnant mothers who broke down crying while they were interviewing a witness. There was a pretty good chance she'd never be taken seriously as a prosecutor ever again if she did. Her colleagues and opponents would bring it up for the rest of her life if she cried in open court.

As Victoria worked, she realized that the baby would seriously affect what she did. She knew Smith had been right about that when he spoke to her, but it didn't hit her until then.

Over the course of her career, she had built up a reputation that gave her respect from her colleagues and judges who knew she could do her job well. Even the workers in the DA's office treated her with dignity because of what she got done and her track record for getting some of the worst criminals off of the streets.

What would those people think of her if she couldn't do her job because of a sick child or having to go to a parent-teacher conference? Was there even anyone who would be as dedicated as she was to her job?

That's why the Chicago position still was a possibility. She wanted to be somewhere she could make a difference in the community and make the city a better place for upstanding citizens to live. If she was the DA, she could do even more good with her position than she could ever do as an ADA.

Maybe now that she and Andrei were in a better place, he'd be up for discussing it again. After all, it was his child, too. But it was her body and her life that had to adapt to everything and deal with the repercussions of the decisions she made.

Even if she did accept the position, by the time she moved to Chicago and got settled in, she'd have to consider time for maternity leave. Maternity leave could last for months, and she wasn't the kind of person who could just sit and stare at a wall all day. Having her ankle keep her down was torture, especially when Andrei wasn't around to pick her up and carry her around.

Most jobs required that employees work from six months to a year before taking time off. She vaguely remembered some sort of time requirements for the FMLA. How would she deal with that knowing all the work she could be doing while at home? The last thing she ever wanted was for her child to feel like he came second to her law career, but she'd never really thought about how having a family would change her life because she never saw that as her future. She was single and happy until Andrei swept her off of her feet. Even though her time with Andrei had been intense and passionate, everything had happened so fast that there was no time to consider what a future with him would even look like.

Maybe the Chicago job was more out of reach than she expected. Yes, she knew Andrei had two daughters, who she was more nervous to meet than she cared to admit, but she couldn't put her entire life on hold because of that...could she?

Whether she moved or not, she had to start thinking like a mother and less like the single, professional woman she was so used to and comfortable with. There was the whole need to find childcare, new doctors, and a search for more family-friendly place to raise her baby in. The more she thought about it, the more overwhelming everything seemed. It made her anxious and uneasy, two emotions she wasn't used to dealing with on a regular basis.

The day passed by fast, and she looked up after

hearing a knock on her door. Andrei stood there in his sexy glory, looking like a god with good taste for Italian suits.

"What are you doing here?" she asked.

"I told you I was taking you to lunch." A smile played on his lips and she fought back the urge to stare at the same mouth that had done some of the most exquisite things to her the night before. More than once. She shivered just thinking about how he had made her feel.

She spotted some of the employees staring at him in the hallway. "Close the door, or people will see you."

His smile shifted into a smirk. "Are you embarrassed to be seen with me?" He winked at her and obviously didn't care about her shyness.

Victoria jumped up and went over to close the door herself. "It's not that," she said, pressing her back up against the door. "You are not exactly unknown around here. Your family's law firm has been pretty popular lately. Plus, I think some of them already suspect I have more than just a professional relationship with you, especially if Deedee said anything to any one of them. Love that girl, but she can get chatty if given the time."

"So? For all they know, I could be here to meet with you about a client."

She stared up at him, and the warmth in his eyes was evident. Any human being who had a sex drive would know what that look meant. "From the way you're looking at me, I think you're making it pretty obvious that you aren't here on business."

"I can't help it. When you look as yummy as you do, I'm going to enjoy it. Any man in his right mind would." He moved in on her, pressing her up against the door, trapping her between the wood and his hard, muscular body.

"Andrei, I'm at work."

"The door is closed." His fingers slid under the hem of her dress. "I can think of at least ten naughty things I could do to you right now." He slid the skirt part up over her hips.

She could feel the hardness of him pressing up against her leg, and a sigh escaped her. She felt wanton and needy, almost as if it had been longer than hours since the last time together.

"You need to stop," she whispered. "Anyone could come in and catch us." The prospect of getting caught just excited her more, if the flush in her cheeks meant anything.

He reached up and turned the lock on our door. "Now that is no chance of that happening." His finger slipped past her panties and found her opening for she could say anything else.

"Oh, God." His two fingers slipped into her easily, and her head fell back against the door with a thunk.

"I love how wet and ready you are for me. Makes it so easy to take you." He moved his fingers in and out of her with ease, working her body in the way only he knew how to do.

"They'll know what we're doing." Although so many excuses filled her head, like the fact that the people outside could probably hear what was going on, she didn't want him to stop. She clenched harder around him, urging his fingers deeper inside. Whenever he touched her like that, with such confidence, she couldn't deny him and never wanted to.

"They'll only know if you make a sound," he said. "I recommend being very quiet." He kissed her into silence.

She couldn't think properly when he kissed her. It was like she forgot how to do anything but respond to him. She was melting inside. He kissed her as his tongue found hers, teasing her. He tasted like cinnamon and that only pushed her closer to him.

A finger found her clit and made slow circles that had her panting.

"Andrei," she moaned.

He shushed her with another kiss. "Careful," he whispered. "You don't want your coworkers to find out the things I'm doing to you right now...unless you're into exhibitionism."

She bit down on her lip to keep from saying anything else or making anymore sounds. He shimmied her underwear down her legs and lifted her feet to slide them off completely. As he stood, he made sure he kept in contact with her as he bunched them in front of his nose. "You smell so fucking good." He stuffed them in his jacket pocket.

"What are you doing?"

"I'm saving it for later. It's going to be a while before I can get you home and have a proper taste, so this will have to keep me satisfied until then."

"You have me now."

"For a quick moment only, but I'm going to make up for lost time later."

She heard his zipper lower before he lifted her up, so she could wrap her legs around him.

"I'll take the short time with you over not being inside you at all." He nudged her opening with the tip of his cock and wasted no time spearing through her in one fluid motion.

Victoria bit down on his covered shoulder to keep from crying out. She couldn't stop a little moan from escaping. She held on tight to him as he moved in and out of her with a rhythm that nearly drove her insane. Her pussy jerked around him, feeling every part of his length.

Although they were both fully clothed except for where they connected, the idea of possibly getting caught and knowing people were on the other side of the door made their lovemaking even more erotic and tantalizing. Her orgasm built up in the pit of her stomach and grew with each thrust Andrei gave. She could feel her wetness, making way for him as he grew thicker inside of her.

Every inch of her body craved him and never wanted him to stop. The growing orgasm became a tangible thing inside of her until it exploded like a firework and spread throughout her body. She crumbles around him as he chained to the inside of her, coming so hard that it broke out another orgasm she didn't expect.

Colors streaked behind her closed eyes as she gripped him tight, never wanting to let go. When she opened them again, he looked at her satisfied grin.

"I'll never get tired of doing," he said. "I'll never get tired of you."

She kissed him with all the strength she had left in her, knowing full well the feeling was mutual.

When they left her office, she felt like everyone who looked their way knew what they did. Even though she was a little paranoid, she was just happy that they left without her boss seeing them.

They didn't go far for lunch. Instead, they ate at a steakhouse Andrei liked that was around the corner from where she worked. He said it was one of his favorites, and she had no intention of arguing with him.

She didn't even complain when Andrei ordered lunch for both of them, a T-bone steak for him and grilled pesto chicken for her, along with baked potatoes and a side salad.

"That's a lot of food for lunch," she said after the waitress left them.

"You know that my beloved child is not going to starve, my love," he said. "Not while I'm around to ensure that baby grows up strong and healthy."

Victoria didn't know how to process everything he said. If it had been any other time, she would have been upset with him taking so many liberties about what she ate, but what kept her silent the most was how he said the word love. Did that mean he loved her? Or was it like when a waitress called you honey?

That was the problem with having the mind of a lawyer. She was used to always over-analyzing things, even the simple ones. He just used the word love. It wasn't like he actually said he loved her.

She didn't know how to take it. From the way he said it, Andrei probably didn't even know the word had slipped from his lips.

A man next to them had ordered raw oysters, and the smell of them made Victoria and queasy. She covered her mouth.

"Oh, God," she thought! "Please don't let me puke in this restaurant in front of Andrei."

When their waiter returned, she asked, "May I have a glass of ginger ale with a lot of ice please? Quickly."

The woman looked a little confused, but she still hurried off to get a drink.

Andrei looked at her with concern in his eyes. "Are you okay? What's wrong?"

"I am fine." She glanced over to the other table with the oysters, and Andrei followed her direction. "Just a little nauseated."

The ginger ale arrived just in time. She gulped it down like it was the last drink she would ever have. She took deep breaths so she didn't get sick.

"Can you move us to another table?" Andrei asked. "My girlfriend's pregnant, and I think the smells around us are getting to her."

She had never been more grateful to him and she was not moment, and she got an odd thrill at being called his girlfriend. They'd never talked about labels before or what exactly they were to each other. They were just taking it in stride.

"Of course, sir," the waitress said. She left briefly and came back. "Right this way."

They moved through the restaurant and followed her. That's when Victoria noticed a few other patrons staring at them. She couldn't help but wonder if it was because they were being moved through the restaurant, or if people stared because she and Andrei were an interracial couple. She hoped it was the first, because the second didn't sit well with her at all.

They had never been on a date before, at least not a public one. New York was a diverse place. Interracial couples weren't hard to spot, but uneasiness still settled in her chest.

After they sat down in a private booth, the waitress asked, "Is that better, ma'am?"

"Yes, thank you." She waited until the woman left before she spoke to Andrei again. "Thank you for doing that."

"Anything for you," he said.

"So I'm your girlfriend, huh?"

"Did I say that?" His tone jested with her.

"I'm pretty positive that's what you said."

"Is that a bad thing?"

"I haven't decided yet, but I like the sound of it, boyfriend."

"I like you calling me that, too. Maybe we should

try it out more often." He flashed a grin at her that showed off his white, even teeth.

It sounded a little silly as she said it. After all, they were having a child together. There should've been a better time to call someone that less juvenile than boyfriend, more serious than baby daddy, and not as binding as husband. Husband. She wondered what kind husband Andrei would be, and if she even had the ability to be wife material. He might never want to marry again after his acrimonious divorce.

Their meal arrived before she could pick that apart like she did everything else. The food looked amazing, and she hoped nothing made her feel sick again. After sampling her food, she knew that wasn't going to be a problem. She didn't realize how hungry she was until she took the first bite, but her stomach gurgled.

Andrei began to eat, too, and it was fun to watch attack his steak like a man on a mission. The way he ate was an erotic event that she could enjoy over and over again without ever getting bored.

Victoria giggled as he devoured another bite. Andrei noticed how she was watching him.

"What's wrong?" he asked.

"Nothing. I just didn't think I would enjoy watching you eat as much as I am."

"I'm glad you're enjoying yourself," he said. "But I have a secret to admit?"

"Oh? What's that?"

"I enjoy eating you a lot more."

Heat filled her cheeks, and she glanced around to make sure no one else heard them. "After last night, I'm certain that's no longer a secret."

He winked at her, and she laughed like a schoolgirl. Whatever Andrei was doing to her, she was starting to love it way more than was probably healthy for her.

She was able to get through half of her meal before nausea hit her again. She wiped her mouth with her napkin before putting it back down.

"Baby, you don't look well?"

Victoria put her hand over her mouth, stood up, and ran to the bathroom. She barely made it to a stall before she hurled. She wasn't even far along and already the baby was wreaking havoc on her body.

Andrei was outside of the women's restroom when she came out and led her back to the table. When she returned, she asked the waitress to wrap her meal up for home.

She thought Andrei looked a little upset. "I'm sorry. I didn't mean to spoil lunch."

"It's not that. I hate that you're going through so much. If not for that baby..."

His voice sounded so harsh that she felt the need to defend it. "It isn't the baby's fault. We are the ones who didn't use protection."

"I know that. The fault is mine though. After two kids, you would think I'd know better."

Victoria didn't like the way this conversation was headed. "Know better? Know better than to have sex with me?"

"That's not what I mean, and you know it. Stop trying to put words in my mouth that aren't there."

"I think I have to. Sounds like you think this baby is mistake."

"Well, we sure as hell didn't plan it."

The waitress brought back the check, but Andrei grabbed it before she could.

"Don't you dare," he said. "I'm paying for this."

The waitress scattered away without saying anything, avoiding the attention that was growing between them.

"I can pay for my own lunch, Andrei. I'm a big girl."

"I know you are, and I have no doubt that you can take care of yourself, but that decision is not yours anymore. Not with my baby inside of you."

"Stop calling it your baby. It's my baby to, and it's my body."

He stared hard at her. "What the fuck is that supposed to mean? I hope not thinking about doing something stupid. Because if you are thinking about getting rid of it, you better stop right now."

Fury filled her. "No! I can't believe you think I'd do something like that. Even if I did, that's not your choice to make."

"The hell it isn't. I know I'm still not sure about this—"

"Not sure? Andrei, this is happening whether we want it to or not." She had to go before she made a scene by doing something like throwing her leftover ginger ale in his face. "I have to get back to work."

"Fine, but you're coming over to my place tonight."

"I don't think so."

"You didn't eat lunch, and I'm almost certain you won't eat dinner if I don't make sure you sit down for a real meal. That's why I am cooking something you can eat without getting sick. You're coming over." He said it with such finality and command that she didn't know how to respond.

She tried to walk away, but he had enough cash for the food and tip. He was right on her heels.

She stopped before they got near her building and

turned to face him. "I can get back to work on my own," she said, her voice cold.

He was already tall and overbearing, but it seemed like he overshadowed her even more with his stern gaze and unmoving posture. "I'm not leaving your side until you promise you'll be at my place tonight."

"Andrei—"

"Do you want me to come upstairs with you and walk you to your office?"

"No!"

"How about show up at your place? We both know I can knock hard until you open up. Your neighbors may be a little upset at the noise, but if that's what it takes..."

"Fine!" she forced out. "I have to go to my place first to at least get some clothes."

"I'll be waiting," he said. He took her off-guard by pulling her to him and kissing her.

When he touched her, it didn't matter that she couldn't stand him. Her traitorous body still reacted to him. Her nipples were hard from his simple kiss.

When he pulled away, he smiled with his victory. This time, it wasn't so charming. He was so cocky and sure of himself; he knew what he could do. She hated it even more because it was still sexy as hell. Even though her mind was angry, her body still wanted him. She was mad at herself for that.

"If I don't hear from you by seven, I'm coming over."

She groaned out her frustration and stormed off before she could do something violent they both would regret and possibly get her arrested.

CHAPTER 16

VICTORIA

VICTORIA WASN'T in the mood to just obey Andrei. He needed to know that she needed to be respected. Even though he went all possessive on her earlier, she was still going to use her leverage as any smart counsel would. Sure, she still packed her overnight things like she told him and even got to his place at one minute past seven, and he called just like she thought he would.

"Hi, Andrei," she said calmly after answering.

"Where are you, Victoria."

"Still packing." She smiled, imaging him pacing and getting riled up.

"You were supposed to be here by now. It's after seven."

"Is it? I must have lost track of time."

"I'm coming over."

"No one can stop you from doing what you have to do. We're both adults."

He opened the door to find her standing in her doorway.

She ended her cell phone call and put it in her pocket. "Like I said, adults can do whatever they want." She pushed past him with a big smile on her face.

He shut the door and "I suppose you think that's funny."

"No. What's funny is that you think you can command me like some lapdog and I'll come running whenever. If this relationship is going to work, you have to treat me with more respect than that."

"I can think about a couple occasions when you didn't mind my demands."

She stared at him, and she immediately thought of the way he commanded her whenever they had sex. "That's not the same thing. Focus."

"Oh, I'm focused." He moved over to the kitchen.

She saw the food spread out on his counters. It looked like a pot of broth was boiling on the stove. "Were you seriously coming after me with food cooking like that? Didn't you think about the apartment burning down?"

"Honestly, when it comes to you, I never think at all. I just act."

He said it so casually that it shocked her. She didn't know she affected him that way until he said it. What could she say?

"Are you telling me I make you irrational?"

"I don't think rational would be the word I'd use, but I don't regret ever being with you."

"Even if it means having a baby we weren't expecting?"

"I admit that having another child scares me, but that doesn't mean that I'd never want be with you."

"I'm still considering Chicago."

She just said it. For some sadistic reason, she was in a mood to test him and his limits. It made no sense why. Maybe she wanted to see what he'd be like angry and if he was bearable to stand. She'd been with a guy who had anger management problems before, and she'd dumped him before he ever got the chance to lay a hand on her.

Deep down, she knew Andrei would never hurt her. She'd seen men who hurt women numerous times as she sent their asses to jail for battering their wives and terrorizing their children. Those weren't men. Real men would never lay a hand on a woman or child.

Even though Andrei had the ability to get on her last nerve, she knew he'd never lay a hand on her or their child. It was something about the protectiveness in his eyes that always lingered there.

"Chicago? I thought we talked about this already."

"No, you told me you had children, and we never finished the conversation. There was a lot we didn't get around to."

"You can't go to Chicago, Victoria."

"There was never a question of whether I could not. You said you couldn't go."

"You weren't having my baby then, but you are now. I think that changes things."

"I hate to break it to you, but pregnant women are in Chicago, too." At first, she had only planned to talk about the baby, but now it seemed like the baby and the promotion intermingled. They were two major parts of her future. One was highly likely and the other was optional. If she chose to take the job in Chicago, her life would change dramatically. Although he didn't say it, she could tell the Andrei still thought it was overwhelming to have a baby right now. She didn't disagree with that, but she still had to at least consider her future, whether it involved him or not.

"I know pregnant women live in Chicago, but that doesn't mean you have to go there. Promotions are important. I get that, I'm sure there will be plenty of opportunities for you to find something like that better here. You're a damn good lawyer, Victoria. That won't be your only chance."

Even with his compliment, she only heard one thing: he was shutting down the promotion before she could really consider it. It wasn't his decision to make. "Maybe working with your father has you a little jaded, but DA positions don't just come out of thin air. In order for me to even get a position like that here, my boss would have to either retire or die. Are you saying I should sit around and wait for something like that to happen?"

"Don't be ridiculous. I never would suggest something like that. All I'm saying is that you should consider your options. There may be other DA positions in the New York area or even some of the surrounding cities. It's already stressful enough to move to a new city alone to start over."

"You think I can't do it, don't you?"

"I couldn't believe that even if I tried to. You are a strong woman. There's no question about that, but who says you have to go all the way to Chicago to prove that?"

"The difference is that none of those positions come with Smith's recommendation. Something like that means a lot and can mean the difference between starting out fresh or beginning a position that has a lot of weight to it. I don't want Smith to think I'm taking this lightly."

"So you want to take my child several states away from me just to please your boss?"

"It's not even a child yet. I'm only four weeks pregnant. In the first trimester, there's a high risk of miscarriage. We have months before this even impacts you. I get you can't leave your children behind here and move with me, but that's you. I'm talking about me, and I have to at least think about myself and my future in all of this."

Victoria was worried it would come to this. It was one of the things that bothered her when Andrei found out about the baby. Most women probably worried that their guy would pack up and leave town to get away from them. Her problem was the exact opposite.

Andrei was stressed out about the possibility that she could leave him and take the new job, making it difficult for him to see the baby.

"That's just it. This stops being about you second

you got pregnant. There is no you anymore. There is only us."

Guilt filled her gut for hassling Andrei about going away to Chicago. For most of her life, she only had to worry about herself. No other lives had to be considered, which meant she always chose the decision that was best for her. But she couldn't push away the words Andrei was trying to get through to her. Victoria's life was no longer her own. Maybe she was being selfish, but did a baby mean she had to give up her dream?

He placed a bowl of broth in front of her.

She quirked an eyebrow up. "What's this?"

"It's a family recipe. My mother made this all the time and she was pregnant with us. It should help with the nausea allow you to get some food down."

The delicious smell of the broth invaded her senses and reminded her that she hadn't eaten much all day.

"Try it," he said.

"What if I can't keep it down?"

"Just try it."

Their talk of Chicago and the baby still floated around her in her head, but she didn't argue with him on this because she was starving.

She took the spoon into a liquid and brought to her lips. A burst of hearty flavor filled her mouth and satisfied her taste buds. Although she couldn't place the specific flavors in the recipe, it suits her stomach as she took a spoonful of more and more until she had almost finished the entire thing.

"I'll take that as a sign that you like it." The corner of Andrei's mouth slid up into a half smile. "Let me get you some more." He took her full and refilled it before she could ask him to.

Andrei confounded her in more ways than one. He was drop-dead gorgeous and the ruthless defense attorney in the courtroom. The man was also the best lover she ever had, putting her needs before his own. Now, he was taking care of her again without her having to ask. Any woman would be crazy not to want him, so why was she so set on pushing him away?

A future in Chicago seemed like the safer option,

far away from her passionate and sometimes mystifying lover.

"We have to figure this out," she said as he put the newly refilled bowl of broth in front of her. "The problem isn't going away just because we stop talking about it."

"I know. Eat your soup."

She downed this bowl a little slower than the first. The whole time Victoria knew that he watched her as she ate. With anyone else, she would've found such scrutiny creepy. This, however, seemed peaceful and homey, more domestic than she was used to but still comforting all the same.

Every once in awhile, she will look up to find him grinning back at her, but she didn't question it or tease him. She simply ate quietly as he continued to watch her every movement.

"I want you to meet my family," he said all of a sudden.

She nearly choked on her last spoonful of broth. "Meet your family?"

"Yeah. One weekend a month we go to the main

house outside of the city to eat and have some time away. Would you like to spend the weekend with us?"

"You don't just want me to meet your family. You want me to spend the weekend with them?"

"You make it sound like something bad. I think the meeting would be great, Victoria."

"Would your family be okay with a stranger coming?"

"You're not a stranger. At least you won't be when you meet them. I think it's about time. You are having my baby, after all. It makes sense to meet them. You'll get the chance to see where I grew up."

She didn't think about the family that came along with Andrei. Hers was all the way on the other side of the country in California. Andrei's worked with him. "You don't think it's too soon?"

That grin she was getting used to returned. "Oh, you want to wait until after the baby is born? Is that it?"

"No, Mr. Smart Ass. It just seems so sudden."

"You think I have a smart ass?" he asked, laughter hinting under his voice.

"This soup is about five seconds from being over your head."

He held his hands up in defense. "No need to get violent. Just appreciating the compliment."

"What if they don't like me?" She hated the insecurities that bubbled to the surface. That's why she loved being a lawyer. She never had to worry about being good enough because she knew what she was doing and what her winning meant to help others. That gave her more than enough confidence to do her job as ADA and do it well. Outside the courtroom was another matter entirely.

"I can tell you right now my mother and sister will love you as much as I do."

"Did you just admit that you love me?"

"Yeah, I guess I did."

"You are really bad at being subtle."

"Fine. Let me make it as obvious as possible. I love

you, Victoria Bellamy. More than I thought it was possible to love and the other human being. I love you, and there is nothing you can do to stop me from ever loving you."

Words usually came easy to her. They had to, or she would make a poor prosecutor, but for the life of her, she didn't know what to say to Andrei.

"Don't say anything now. I don't want you to say anything you don't mean. But I can promise you one thing, Victoria, I'm not going to rest until I hear you say it back to me. That's a promise, and I always keep my promises."

He took her bowl away to refill it once more before she could say anything at all. One thing was certain. Andrei was getting more complicated by the day, and he was going to be an interesting puzzle to figure out.

CHAPTER 17

ANDREI

ANDREI WOKE up to the smell of sex and bacon. The first he knew the origin of because he could smell it all over his room, and he loved it. He loved her, and he made sure she knew that fact last night. He couldn't think of how his room smelled before she was in it, and he never wanted it to go back to how it was in the past.

The second smell of food had him up and throwing his pajama bottoms on. He hunted his way into the kitchen until he found her at his stove, trying to cook. He knew she said cooking wasn't her thing, but she still looked beautiful moving that sweet ass of hers in his kitchen...an ass he loved fondling in and out of bed.

He leaned over the bar, entranced by her delicious

curves that he only sampled a few hours before, but already he wanted more of her. She was his drug, and he didn't mind being addicted. Not if it meant waking up to this lovely sight it every morning.

He eyed the semi-burnt toast and the mounds of what looked like eggs, while she worked on the bacon and sausage that had lured him out of his sleep.

She turned around and jumped.

"Morning," he said. "I didn't mean to scare you. I hate to pull you out of your morning element, especially one that is a pleasure to watch."

"You mean a morning nightmare," she said. "I know I ruined the toast, and I'm not even sure the eggs Benedict is edible. I don't even know that should be classified as eggs. I wanted to make you breakfast in bed, but it took longer than I thought. The only things that may be salvageable are the bacon and sausage. Oh, and definitely the coffee and possibly the fried apples, but I won't be disappointed if you sample it all with caution. I can't guarantee nothing will explode in your mouth when you eat it."

"Explosions and death by a great-smelling breakfast. Either way, it still sounds like a feast fit for a king. Aren't I the one who should be making you an apology breakfast after last night?"

She smiled. "You've already made me breakfast before, remember? One much more edible than this."

Oh, he remembered. Damn. Was that really only a few weeks ago? He couldn't believe time had passed so quickly, but it felt like they'd been together so much longer than that.

"I wanted to at least try to do something nice for you, but honestly, you may be better off eating poison or anything else suitable for rats."

"Come on. It doesn't look that bad." He moved around the counter and kissed her as she held the spatula. He took it from her and moved the sausage and bacon around to keep them from burning. He finally took a quick bite of her eggs. He chewed the bland eggs and crunched on pieces of shell, but he swallowed it all in one gulp. "See? Not bad at all."

"Really?" she asked. He could hear the hope in her

voice. He thought about lying, but he'd told her he'd be honest with her.

"All it needs is a little more salt and a lot less shell."

"I knew I missed some of those little, fragile suckers. How the hell do you do this on a regular basis without killing yourself and others?"

He couldn't help but laugh and pull her into his arms.

"What's so funny?" she asked.

"I'm laughing at how serious you get about breakfast," he said. "You'd think you were prepping a deposition."

"Trust me. Depositions are a piece of cake compared to this. I wanted it to be perfect."

"It is because you made it."

"You smooth-talking me isn't going to make my cooking any better or turn me into Betty Crocker."

"Then you'll just have to come over here more often so we can get it right together."

"Careful," she said. "That sounds like you're asking me to move in or something."

He thought about it and did something he'd never done before. He grabbed the little container in one of his utility drawers and handed it to her.

"What is this?" she asked.

Andrei wrapped his arms back around her, right where they belonged. "Open it."

She undid the small box and looked inside before staring up at him. "It's a key."

"That's what it looks like," he teased. "Yep. I'm absolutely certain that's the shape of a key."

"This isn't a key to what I think it is, right?"

"If you're thinking it's a key to this place then you'd be correct in that assumption, prosecutor."

"I can't move in with you, Andrei."

"Why not? It sounds perfectly reasonable to me. I don't have to wait for you to come over, because you'll already be here."

"We barely know each other."

"There are people who move in within a few days of meeting each other. I'm sure we've got them beat by seeing each other longer."

"I can't move in. Not right now when I don't even know if I'm staying in New York."

Andrei hated hearing her mentioning moving. He wanted her to stay right there with him so he could wake up to seeing her ruin breakfast more often.

"Then don't think of it as moving in just yet," he said. "Think of it as a key for you to keep for now. You know, in case you want to come over or spend the night. Now, you don't have to wait for me to come home. Just come in. Besides, we know each other better than you want to believe. I have every inch of your mesmerizing body committed to memory."

"You knowing how to do wickedly good things to me in bed doesn't mean we understand everything about each other."

"Really? I beg to differ." He nuzzled her neck and planted a light kiss on her throat.

"This is insane."

"I don't think so. I already have your apartment key from when I stayed over. Let's just call it a legitimate swap."

"It's just a lot, you know?"

"Victoria, eventually you're going to have step back and let people help you sometimes. It doesn't make you weak or any less capable, so can you stop fighting and just let me do this, Okay."

She seemed too exhausted to fight him, so she said, "Okay."

"Good. Now, about your next doctor's appointment. Maybe you should consider going to my family's office."

"You mean your mother and sister's practice?"

"Of course. They're some of the best doctors in the state. I can at least feel more comfortable than when a man gets to see and touch places that are just for me."

"You'll be comfortable. I don't think so. That is not happening. Ever. You already want me to meet your family. I'm not having your mother and sister probing me. Even thinking about that creeps me out. I can imagine the awkward dinner talk about birthing processes and vaginal health. That's where I draw the line, Andrei."

He started to say something, but she put a finger on his lips.

"You get one big change a week, mister. I took your key, so I'm keeping my doctor."

He sighed but relented to her choice, since he didn't want her handing his key back. If she tried giving that back, he'd find a way to sneak it back into her purse somehow. His woman wasn't getting off that part easy. "Fine. When do you go back to the doctor? I'm coming with you."

Her eyes widened. "You don't have to do that."

"I know I don't have. I want to.

"I'm a big girl, Andrei. I don't need you to go to my doctor appointments with me."

Andrei pulled her close and kissed her, hard and certain so she could stop thinking so much. She tasted so warm and lovely that it was hard for him to stop kissing her, but he pulled her back. He enjoyed that dazed look she had on her face, and he loved it even more that he was responsible for putting it on there. "I'm coming, and that's final. You can either give me the information now, or I'll find out on my own, Victoria." He grabbed his phone just to show that he wasn't playing around. He'd never joke around when it came to her or their baby.

She told him, and he put it in his phone to make sure he wouldn't forget. He wasn't missing that appointment since he wanted to make sure the doctor knew what the fuck he was doing. If the guy turned out to be an idiot, he was going to find her another doctor who treated her right. Just because she decided not to use his family's services didn't mean she was going to be making decisions alone. He was going to be right there through all of it.

Andrei was starving, and with a few changes, he and Victoria were able to salvage breakfast. He made Victoria some of the leftover broth for lunch and made her promise him that she'd eat it and not something else that would make her sick.

At work, he wasn't able to do as much as he should, because he was worried about her and what his parents would say about their relationship.

He called his mother first, since she was the most welcoming in the family. His mother didn't have a mean bone in her body, which contrasted with his father's strong personality. But their relationship worked, and they were happy together. That's what he wanted with Victoria. Even though they clashed in more ways than one, the woman was a permanent part of his system.

His mother picked up after the second ring. "Hi, honey. What a lovely surprise. I rarely get a call from you or your brother anymore."

"I'm sorry, mom. I know I should check in more often."

"Hell must have frozen over and collapsed into itself," another voice called out. Of course his mother had put him on speaker phone with his sister there. "He never calls us anymore."

"That's not true, Amy. I call when I can.

"Yeah? When was the last time?" Amy asked.

"I can't remember the exact date."

"Just because you see Dad and Sam everyday doesn't mean you can skip out on us, dork."

"Whatever you say, monkey." He smiled at how easy it was to talk to his mother and sister.

"It's a slow day for us," his mother said. "Yesterday we delivered triplets, so I guess it's good to have a breather. Now, do we get a reason for this unexpected surprise call?"

"I'm bringing someone home next weekend, and I really want you all to meet her. I just wanted to make sure that's okay with you." Andrei felt his nerves rattle some. In court, he was ice cold, but his family sometimes had him on edge, more his father than anyone else.

"Are you kidding? That's wonderful, honey."

He could almost see his mother's smile on the other end, and he took a breath.

"Anyone's better than the last one you brought home."

The last one was his ex-wife, who he didn't want to even think about at the moment.

"No bashing," his mother said. "Even if Trish's difficult, she's still the mother of my grandchildren.

Speaking of those two, I hope you're bringing them, too."

"I am," he said. "I want Victoria to meet everyone, but I'm just worried it'll be a lot for her."

"Don't worry, Andrei. We'll make sure she feels welcome the whole time."

"Thanks, Mom, but it's not you I'm worried about."

"Your father will be fine. Have you told him yet?"

"I wanted to tell you first, but I'm going to tell him and Sam next."

"Whatever you father says, don't let it get to you. I will make sure he's on his best behavior."

"Thanks," he said. "I'll need the reinforcements." Even though his father had his moments, he always listened to his wife and treated her with love and respect.

"I'll have to plan the meal," his mother said. "We should have roast turkey with rice, mushrooms, and butternut squash. Oh and there's this stuffed pepper recipe I have wanted to try as well as a sweet potato pie one."

"He doesn't need to hear the entire menu," Amy complained.

Andrei laughed. Their mother was the one he'd got the cooking bug from for a reason. "Whatever you fix will be great, Mom. It always is, and I'm sure Victoria will love it. She's not picky and knows great food when she tastes it."

"Her name's Victoria. I'm so excited to meet her. I can't wait, dear."

"I may bring Erik, too. I think we both could use some time out of the city, and since he doesn't have any family here, the mini vacation may do him some good."

"Sure. We always love having, Erik. I have to go and start planning everything."

"Good going, dork. You've unleashed the cooking beast again. Don't forget who she drags in to help her with all these cooking and baking plans."

"Oh hush, Amy," his mother said. "It'll be good for us. I have to get some things ready. We'll see you all Friday for dinner."

"Okay. We will see you then." When Andrei hung

up, he felt more confident about telling his father, knowing that his mother would have his back at least.

He told his brother to meet him in their father's office and took a deep breath before leaving his. As usual, his father was huddled over massive amounts of paperwork.

Andrei knocked on the open door to get his attention. "Dad, do you have a minute?" he asked.

"Can it wait until later?" his father asked without looking up. "I'm working on a deadline for a client here."

"It'll be quick."

"Fine." He put the paper he was reading down and looked up at Andrei. "What is it then?"

His father was a kind man when he wanted to be, but work had the tendency to stress the man out. Although he had built a multi-million dollar firm, the money came with more responsibility and stress that had his father on edge most of the time. The man wanted Andrei to be more like his brother, Sam, who lived and breathed law since he was made to follow in their father's footsteps. Andrei wished Sam had been born first to take the pressure off him to be a lawyer, but there were still times he enjoyed the profession.

Working as a chef had no guarantees as a lawyer, and at least he was able to provide for his daughters. Now, he just had to convince Victoria to let him take care of her every once in awhile, too. The woman was stubborn, but he had some tactics on how to get her to see his way that involved a lot of bedroom time and pampering during her pregnancy.

"You called," Sam said, popping his head in.

"Come in," Andrei said. "I just wanted to let both know I'm bringing someone special to the house this weekend."

"When did you start seeing someone?" Sam asked.

"We've been seeing each other for some time now." He didn't want to hear his father's speech on him barely knowing Victoria, so he left the exact time out.

"This isn't the same girl we were talking about before. That prosecutor?"

Andrei nodded, unashamed. "It's her. You're going to have to get used to her, Dad. We're together now."

"How do you think this is going to look for our law firm, son?"

"Frankly, I don't care. I'm with her. I just thought I'd give you the courtesy of letting you know before I brought her to the house this weekend."

"The weekend?" his father asked.

"That's right, and I already cleared it with Mom." He smiled. "I'll let you get back to work. I know that you're busy." He left before his father could object to anything else. Once he knew his mother approved, his father usually backed off.

Sam followed on his heels. "You're really doing this, huh?"

His brother knew at least something about the issue he had with Judge Hughes and Victoria, but he didn't push Andrei about it.

"I am. You don't have a problem with that, do you?"

His brother patted him on the back. "Not at all. I am just happy to get some entertainment this weekend."

Andrei shook his head. He hoped like hell the entertainment stayed limited to the television and music. Anything else could be too much for Victoria to handle, and he wasn't going to let his family scare her off.

It was still hard for Andrei to work without thinking about Victoria. He knew she worried about meeting his family, but they were important to him, especially his daughters. His ex-wife Trish was going to be an annoyance. She always was when he wanted his girls to go to family weekend, probably because Trish wasn't a part of it anymore.

He wanted Victoria to meet his girls, and family weekend seemed like a good time to do that, but he put off calling Trish later.

Andrei could sense the tension that still existed between him and Victoria. He'd be a fool not to notice it. He also knew that she still wanted to go to

Chicago, but he saw the time spent with his family as a chance to convince her to stay in New York. He didn't like having her so stressed out while she carried his baby inside of her. He didn't want her stressed at all, but he couldn't stop the immediate feeling to protect her and his baby whenever he thought about them.

He took time to have lunch with Erik. Meeting with Erik always helped him figured stuff out, especially since he wasn't the type of person to fuck around with words. Erik was a good guy who always spoke his mind. If people didn't like it, that was their problem.

Andrei met his best friend at the Little Old Pub for lunch. This pub was quiet with booths and tables for eating and a decent-sized bar for drinking. It was dim lighting throughout, but the televisions on the walls added to some additional lighting.

"What are you boys having today?" a waitress wearing a tight, black tank top and matching shorts asked.

"A double cheeseburger, fries, and a beer please,"

Erik told her. His flirtatious smile and wink were obvious, and the woman giggled.

Erik may have admired the woman, but Andrei's thoughts only had Victoria running through it. The woman has planted herself in Andrei's heart, mind, and life. It wasn't enough though. He still wanted more of her. He was a selfish bastard when it came to her, but he wanted all of Victoria. He had a feeling he wasn't going to satisfied until he got it.

Andrei didn't feel up to perusing for something else. "I'll have the same." He handed the waitress back his menu and waited for to bring their beers before he started talking.

"Thanks for taking time out to see me," Andrei said. "Could use some advice right about now."

"Hey, that's what friends are for, right?" Erik took a gulp of his beer. "You sounded intense on the phone."

Andrei took a drink, too. "Victoria's pregnant."

"Victoria? The same lawyer you were seeing?"

After taking another sip, Andrei nodded. "That's her."

"Pregnant. Damn, you sure didn't waste any time, did you?"

"It must have happened while we were in Montego Bay."

"So you threw protection out the window when you boarded the plane."

"We were in the moment, and we certainly didn't plan on this. It just happened."

"Since you already have two kids, I figured as much. What are you going to do?"

"Nothing to do. She wants to keep it, and I want it. I want her, too. I'm in love with her."

"Well, you seem sure about this."

"I am. I've never been more certain about anything. I know I want her and the baby in my life no matter what."

"Then congratulations! I think it's great. You have a beautiful woman and a baby on the way." He lifted his beer. "Here's to them!"

Andrei lifted his glass, but he wasn't in a celebratory mood.

"What's the problem now?"

"As much as I want her, I think she's having doubts."

"About what?"

"Us. Everything. I gave her a key to my place. She took it, but you should have seen her face. That woman is not used to people taking care of her."

"Just like you're not used to a woman who wants to take care of herself."

"What's that supposed to mean?"

"Trish had moments of being nice, but she was clingy as a leech. Remember that time we were supposed to go to Atlantic City for my birthday? You couldn't go because she didn't want to be in the house alone all weekend. Now, you got to get used to someone who's not like that."

"Where are you going with this?"

"Ease her into this. Although you probably want to watch over her all the time, you may have to slow it down for her. You're moving pretty fast."

"Then I guess you're not going to like what I did before that."

"What else is there, man?"

"I invited her to meet my family next weekend when we go out to the main house. She agreed to that at least."

"So much for going slow." Erik shook his head, but he smiled while doing it. "I've haven't seen you like this before."

"Like what?"

"Happy and a nervous wreck all at once." Erik rubbed his chin. "No. I take that back. I've seen you like this twice before."

"And when was that?"

Erik stared at him, waiting for him to get it.

It didn't take him long to get where his friend was going. "When Asya and Naida were born."

"Bingo. You were a joyful, jittery mess. Couldn't stand you. One minute you were a proud papa and the next you were worried about ruining their lives because of the long work hours you put in. This time is different though."

"Yeah? How so?"

"The way you talk about your new girl, you seem content. You didn't do that with Trish."

"This feels different. Trish and I dated so long that it only made sense to get married. As much as I cared about her, I never felt like this with her."

"Did you tell Victoria that?"

"I told her I loved her."

"That's big, but sometimes that's not enough."

"Saying that was a big deal to me."

"Did she say it back?"

"I could tell I caught her off guard, so I told her I'd wait."

"Losing patience already?"

"I'm not worried about patience. I can wait as long as she wants me to. What I can't do is see her move to Chicago."

"She's still considering it?"

"Apparently she never stopped seeing it as an option."

"Don't let her run away to Chicago. If you don't want her to leave, you have to keep her here."

"How do you suggest I do that?"

"Grand gestures can work."

"I already told her I love her."

"Verbal affirmation isn't a gesture."

"What should I do?"

Erik crossed his arms and waited again.

Andrei quirked his brow when he realized what Erik was getting at. "I thought you said we were moving too fast."

"That was before you told me she could leave for another state. You love her and want both her and the baby."

"I'd do anything for them."

"Then you have your answer. Besides, slow isn't for everyone."

"Okay. I'll do my best to keep her here in New York. There's no question about it. I have to convince her she belongs with me."

"Thatta boy," Erik teased. "Now that's settled, I have a serious question for you."

"Shoot." Andrei leaned forward, expecting something serious.

"Can I finally be Uncle Erik?"

Andrei laughed so hard, he had to grip the table. He needed the break in real talk, because there was no question Erik would be a large part in the kid's life just like his daughters loved Erik."

"Of course you can. Once Victoria meets you, I'm sure she'll agree."

"Good because I love you, man, but having no one sucks ass."

Andrei could understand where Erik was coming from. They'd been best friend since high school, and a car accident had taken his parents just before graduation. That had been a huge blow to him, so Andrei's family had taken him in until he decided to go out on his own. He refused any help and chose to make a life for himself, one that he was happy with until recently.

"Why don't you come next weekend, too?" he asked Erik. "Everyone would be happy to see you, especially the girls." Andrei also knew how much being called Uncle Erik meant. Trish had been dead set against it and wouldn't let their girls call him that. Whenever he asked why, she'd just say it was because he wasn't really their uncle. She'd even denied having Erik as a godfather. He'd have to ask Victoria for her blessing after she met him, which was another good reason to have Erik at the family house.

"You don't think it'll be too crowded?"

"It's never too crowded for you. You're family"

"Thanks." He took a last swig of his beer as the waitress brought out their food. "This reminds me. Your mother will be cooking that amazing food of hers, right?"

Andrei grinned. "Her feast is sure to happen. I'll be

sure to warn her you're coming so we don't end up with an empty table like we've been cleaned out by a plague of locusts."

"Good deal." Erik bit into his burger with a vengeance.

As Andrei ate, he at least appreciated knowing his friend would be there to have his back for family weekend.

NEW YORK WASN'T the best city to drive in, so most people used taxis or public transportation. Victoria usually took a taxi to work because the subway was too crowded for her liking. She had been in one of Andrei's cars before, but she was in too much pain before to actually appreciate it. The one they got in was different then the first. He opened the door of a fancy blue Rolls Royce convertible.

"This isn't the same car you took me to the hospital in," she said as she got inside. "I was hurting, but I'm sure I'd remember this one."

He grinned as he got in the driver's seat. "That was my city car. This is my country car."

The seat molded to her and felt like the most comfortable seat she'd ever sat in. "You are definitely not a state lawyer. This is the private law lifestyle experience all the way."

"What?" Andrei asked, starting the car up, which purred smoothly to life. "You don't like my toys?"

"Let's just say your toys take some getting used to."

It felt so natural riding in the car with Andrei, and it gave her the picture of being a real couple with him. It was something she tried not to think too hard about before, but it was hard to ignore as the rode out of the city. Victoria could feel her stomach tie itself in knots as they set out to the Rusak family home. "Are you sure me coming will be okay?"

"Yes, why wouldn't it be?" Andrei asked.

"I feel like I'm intruding."

"You're with me. They'll be happy to have you there."

"Are your parents going to make us sleep in separate rooms or something?"

"No, my parents are not traditional like that. If

anyone tried to keep me from you, I promise I'd find a way to sneak into your room."

She laughed. "I have no doubt you'd try."

"Besides I think it's too late to keep us from trying something."

"I guess you're right." Victoria said. "Did you tell her about the baby?"

"Not yet. I wanted to wait and tell them with you."

"What do you expect to say? 'This is my girlfriend. Surprise. We're pregnant?'"

"I didn't exactly plan it out, but I think we can do it smoother than that. Everyone will be happy for us. That's all that matters. My mom will be thrilled because she'll have a new baby to spoil."

"Did you tell them that I am black?" Victoria asked.

Andrei paused a while, then finally answered. "No."

"That's kind of important information to leave out. Now they're getting two surprises." The comfortable seat was starting to feel like a trap she couldn't escape. She wiggled around a little, but she didn't have anywhere to go.

"I didn't want to make an issue about it. Something like that doesn't matter to me or them."

"Are you sure about that?"

"I'm sure once my family meets you and sees how happy you make me, it won't matter to them. If anyone makes you feel uncomfortable, we will leave. All right? But that's not going to happen. Have some faith in me."

Andrei calmed her a little, but having faith in people was a little hard for her to do, especially with the crimes she had to deal with on a regular basis. History had showed her people could be selfish and cruel.

But Andrei had asked her to believe in him. Was that so hard for her to do?

"This is meant to be a relaxed time for you to meet them and for them to see why I love you so much. Trust in that." He put his hand on her thigh, and the feel of his warmth steadied her panic until it drifted away with the buildings they passed.

"All right," Victoria asked. "I trust you."

Andrei left out the specifics of the country house. The long driveway was surrounded by trees and flowers to make it seem more like a botanical garden then the entrance to a residence. The so-called house wasn't a house unless you took five or six of them and merged them together to make a country mansion. Behind the house was a lake that looked private since Victoria couldn't see another house in the area.

"This is where you grew up?"

"Yeah, but it's been renovated since then."

"What could you possibly have to renovate?"

"My mother wanted more space, and my father had to comply or feel her wrath."

"I like her already."

A woman opened the mansion door, and Victoria saw an immediate family resemblance.

"Andrei! Finally," she said and hugged him tight.

"Hi, mom," Andrei said. "It's good to be here."

She looked at Victoria and a large smile covered her face, one that was hard to fake. "This must be Victoria." Andrei's mother hugged Victoria so tightly that Victoria could not breathe. The woman smelled like flowers and pie, and for some reason that helped Victoria finally feel relieved at being there.

"You're so beautiful," his mother said. "Come in, and we'll get you settled." She took Victoria's hand and led her through the house as if she'd done it multiple times before already.

Victoria was speechless, but Mrs. Rusak didn't seem to mind that and Victoria didn't try to pull away. When she glanced back, Andrei had their overnight bags, and Victoria saw something she had never seen in him before. Pride. A pride like he enjoyed having her there and that shocked her more than anything.

Sam looked like his and Andrei's father, and the oldest Rusak was the only one who intimidated her some, but after a stern calling out from Mrs. Rusak, the man seemed to soften up some.

"Where's your sister?" Victoria asked, remembering Andrei had two siblings.

"She's on an errand to bring something special soon," Andrei said. "She'll be here soon. Erik should be too."

"He beat you here," Mrs. Rusak said. "That boy can eat. He's been asking if I can give him a sample of the dinner before everyone eats."

"That's because your cooking is so good," a voice said. A tall man came into view, and he looked like he towered over everyone but Andrei and Mr. Rusak.

"Honey, this is my best friend, Erik," Andrei said.

"Awful introduction," Erik said. "But I can do one better." Without warning, Erik lifted Victoria up into a bear hug and swung her around in his friendly embrace."

"Erik, don't break my girl. You may want to give her some personal space and room to breathe."

The Rusak family was one made of huggers, something Victoria's family didn't do often. She admitted to herself she kind of liked the change and ended up laughing by the time Erik put her back down on her feet.

"Sorry. I feel like I know you already."

She smiled up at him. "I don't mind," she said. "It's nice to meet you, Erik."

"Wow. You're more gorgeous than Erik let on. Too polite for his own good too."

"I'll take that as a compliment for her," Andrei said. "Not too sure about me."

"You'll live without a compliment," Erik said.

"If you ate all of Mom's cooking, I can't promise you'll be so lucky. I'm starving."

"The dinner will be ready soon," Mrs. Rusak said.

"Everything smells delicious," Victoria said. Her stomach didn't turn, which made her hopeful she could actually enjoy a regular meal without getting sick.

"Thank you, dear," Mrs. Rusak said. "Why don't you two get your things settled then come back down and join us. Erik, Sam, will you both help me set the table and carry the food to the table?"

"Yes, mom," Sam said.

"Sure, Mrs. Rusak," Erik added as they both followed her into another room.

"Let's take our stuff upstairs to my room. Do you want to come up with me?"

"Miss a chance to see your childhood bedroom? How could I pass that up?" She followed him through the house until he led her up a wide staircase. The place was larger on the inside than it looked on the outside. As they climbed the steps, she saw family pictures on the walls. From private school photos and graduations to family group pictures, the images made her want to get to know Andrei's family more and learn about his past.

When they got to the second floor, they went down a long carpeted hallway that looked beautifully furnished with wooden tables, lamps, and more pictures mixed with art. Even though everything looked expensive, it felt homey and comforting as Victoria walked through the house.

Andrei stopped at a closed door, and Victoria almost ran into him from looking around them as she followed.

"Why'd we stop?" she asked.

"Promise you won't judge me too harshly when you see inside. I haven't changed it much since I left for college years ago. Kind of nostalgic."

"Andrei, open the door."

"Just know I warned you."

With his warning, she expected bats to fly out and attack her. She took her time going in, and the inside of his room shocked her. Instead of finding posters of bands and hot swimsuit models, there was a lot of art on the walls. This wasn't like the commercial pieces she'd seen moments before lining the hallway. The pieces that hung had a more personal feel as if they were done by a local artist.

"Your room is awesome. It's so big and spacious. I was thinking it was going to be atrocious or something from the way you talked about it."

"My mother probably came up and sorted things out, so you wouldn't think I was a pig or something," Andrei said. "We have a housekeeper, but sometimes Mom still insists on doing things herself now and then."

"But your apartment always looks amazing."

"That's because I have a maid," Andrei said as he smiled. "Comes twice a week, although she complains that's not enough for the damage I can do."

Victoria chuckled. "Does that mean she needs to come every day if I moved in?"

"It probably wouldn't hurt. Wait, does that mean you're accepting my offer to stay with me?"

"Let's just say I'm thinking it over. That's it. Don't get your hopes up."

"Too late for that. My hopes are up and aren't coming down until I get an answer." He squeezed her shoulder.

Instead of answering him and disappointing him in the fact that she still wasn't sure it was the best idea, she moved out of his arms and over to some of the pictures.

The drawings varied in nature. She recognized

some New York buildings and landmarks. Most of the others showed drawings of the physical body like hands, feet, the brain, heart and other images that almost looked like they were taken from medical books. What had her interest the most were the artistic drawings of food arranged in creative ways on plates and different arrangements of kitchen items so they created art within art.

One was a simple drawing of female figure, and the detail of her muscles and skin were so realistic, she found herself moving closer to it. She could see the lines of the back and limbs although the face was hidden since it was the back of a woman. At the bottom she saw a signature that made her pause over it longer than she would have without seeing it: A. Rusak.

"Did you draw this?" she asked, moving closer to see the signature.

"I drew all of them."

Victoria took in the entire wall before looking around the room and noticed the same signature on all the drawings. "Wow. You're amazing."

He moved up behind her and held her as she stared

at the collage of drawings filling most of the spaces, some in color and others in black and white.

"They're not the best in the world, but I'm still proud of them."

"I don't understand. You have no artwork in your apartment."

"That's because I stopped not long after I went to college."

"Why would you do that?"

"I wasn't passionate about it anymore. I did all those drawings of the body because I wanted to be a doctor, hence the multiple body and organ pictures. If my head wasn't in a medical book, it was used to perfect the drawings I saw in them. I even interned at a hospital my mother delivered her patients' babies in, and they allowed me to see a few things behind the scenes. That's what I thought my life would be all about."

"You gave that up to go to law school?"

"Yeah."

Victoria turned so she could face him, but she was

glad he didn't let go. "You said before you changed because of your father. Are you passionate about law?"

Andrei stared into her eyes, and she could almost see how he thought about her question before answering.

"I've learned to enjoy it," he finally said.

"That's not the same at being passionate."

"No, but in a way I've still found a way to do something that helps people. I still read medical books and journals when I can. That's enough to satisfy me. Besides, that's not what makes me happy."

"What makes Andrei Rusak happy?"

"Right this moment? That would be you." He leaned down and kissed her tenderly, exploring her mouth with ease and lingering there.

She wrapped her arms around his neck and allowed him to erase their heavy conversation. It made her long for him to explore her bare skin with his hands and let him follow that with his mouth.

Victoria was the one to pull away from the kiss. "As much as I want to be with you, I am not having sex with you in your parent's house."

"They won't disturb us. No one will."

"That's not the point. I am so not having sex with you while your family is in the nearby vicinity."

"You're no fun." He swatted her bottom and took the sting out of his words.

"And I'd be no fun facing your parents after doing naughty things with their son and the potential for them to hear everything."

"What kind of naughty things are we talking about?"

She slapped his arms. "Stop it. I mean it."

"Now that I have you in a good mood, I think I should let you know something else."

"Oh?"

"All of my family will be here this weekend, including Asya and Naida."

"Your daughters will be here?" A new set of nerves hit Victoria. "You want me to meet them?"

"Don't worry. I know they'll love you. I was right about the rest of my family. As soon as they get to know you, they'll be happy."

Victoria felt like the pictures were caving in on her. "I feel a little dizzy."

"You should eat and drink something. We should go back down stairs and find you something before dinner starts."

She let him take her hand and lead her back the way they came.

The ended up in the kitchen, where Mrs. Rusak was putting together a few things for dinner.

"Mom, do you have any ginger ale?" Andrei asked.

"Yes, plenty," she said, looking up briefly.

Victoria sat down at the kitchen table, while Andrei grabbed the ice-cold ginger ale from the refrigerator."

When his mother saw him hand it to her, she asked, "Are you feeling well, dear?"

"She's just a little dizzy," Andrei answered for her. "That's all."

Although his mother nodded, she still eyed Victoria with concern. Although Victoria wasn't showing, she couldn't help but wonder if the woman could see a pregnant sign blinking and pointing to her.

"Mom, have you heard from Amy yet?"

"Yes, she just pulled into the driveway," Mr. Rusak said. "Your daughters are with her." He watched Victoria as if expecting some extreme reaction.

Andrei moved in front of Victoria, blocking his father's view of her. "She knows, Dad, but thanks for trying to start something."

"Be nice to each other. We have guests," Mrs. Rusak said. "Forgive them, Victoria. Sometimes I think my boys work too long together to enjoy a family get-together when we have one."

"It's fine. My family has their moments, too," Victoria said. She took another sip of ginger ale, hoping to be stable enough to meet Andre's daughters and eventually eat with the rest of the family.

"Daddy! Daddy!" Two blurs of little people flew into sight and ran into Andrei.

"There are my two tornados," Andrei said, grabbing both of the figures. "How are my girls doing?"

"We had so much fun at camp today!" the youngest one said.

"You did? What did you do?"

"We made dream catchers, see?" She held up her colorful net with feathers and trinkets swinging down.

"That's beautiful, honey. What about you, Asya? Did you make one, too?"

"She doesn't want to show you hers," Naida said. "Hers broke when she sat on it after Mommy picked us up."

"I'm sorry, sweetie. I'd still love to see it."

The oldest girl pulled out her dream catcher, but the circular net was twisted. "It's all crooked."

"It's still one of the best dream catchers I've ever seen."

Asya smiled at her father's compliment, and that little smile made Victoria want to cry. Damn pregnancy hormones were making her an emotional disaster.

"See," Naida said. "I told you he'd like it."

"I have someone I want you two to meet." Andrei led his daughters over to Victoria.

She sniffled a little, hoping her tears weren't close to the surface. She didn't want to scare the kids as soon as she met them.

Although Victoria wasn't as nervous now that she'd seen them, she was grateful to be sitting down.

"This is Victoria. She's a special person that Daddy really cares about."

Both girls looked at her for what felt like ages. Then the youngest one did something she wasn't expecting. She moved forward and hugged Victoria, making her gasp.

"Hi, I'm Naida," the little girl said.

"It's nice to meet you Naida."

The girl moved back and smiled. "Do you like dream catchers?"

Victoria glanced up at a smiling Andrei, and she got a glimpse at the proud father he'd be for the baby that was growing steadily inside of her.

"I love dream catchers," Victoria said.

"Then here." The girl handed Victoria her dream catcher. "You can have mine. I made it for Daddy, but since he likes Asya's broken one, I don't think he'll mind if you have this one. Right, daddy?"

"Sure, honey." Andrei said and nodded at Victoria.

"That's really sweet of you," Victoria said, taking the girl's gift. "I'll cherish it always."

The little girl chuckled.

"All right, Munchkins," Mrs. Rusak said. "Time for you to get washed up for dinner."

The girls ran out of the kitchen to get ready.

That's when the tears started falling, and Andrei was there with tissues.

"Are you okay?" he asked.

She sniffled and dried her eyes. "It's just so beautiful. I want our baby—"

A utensil clattered to the floor. Victoria realized her slip too late.

"Your baby?" Mrs. Rusak asked. "Are you pregnant, Victoria?"

Victoria looked at Andrei for guidance, and he nodded his head.

There was no use hiding the truth now.

"Yes, ma'am," Victoria said. "I'm pregnant."

"We just found out, Mom," Andrei said.

The woman's smile filled her entire face as she ran over to them and hugged Andrei tight. "I'm going to get another grandbaby?"

"That's right." He allowed his mother to hug him before she turned her sights to Victoria.

She pulled Victoria up and hugged her even tighter than she did earlier. "I know you'll make my son happy. I just know it."

"Well," said Victoria. "I would like a few more minutes to sip on the ginger ale. I still feel queasy."

"Sure, honey," Mrs. Rusak said. "I didn't mean to hug you so tight. Don't worry. You should only be nauseous during the first trimester. After that you will be eating like a starved dog. When I was pregnant with Andrei, I thought that I was going to starve to death. It didn't matter what I ate, I was always hungry. If you're anything like me, you'll eat and sleep. Two of the best things about being pregnant, so be sure to enjoy them now. That reminds me. Andrei, make sure she gets two plates tonight before Erik eats everything."

"I'll make sure she's taken care of, Mom," Andrei said. "No need to worry about that."

Victoria was happy with how Andrei's mother took the news. "I feel better now. I think I can eat."

Mr. Rusak popped his head in the kitchen. "Honey, how much longer will it be. We're famished out here."

"I am sorry," Victoria said. "It's my fault. We had to wait until my nausea went away, so I don't embarrass myself at the table.

"All right," Mrs. Rusak said. "Hold your horses. We are ready to eat."

Everyone sat around the large dining room table and passed the food around. Everything looked spectacular to Victoria. It was more like a feast for an army squadron than a dinner for a family.

Erik sat across from Victoria, and out of everyone, he ate eating faster than anyone else.

"Don't mind him," Andrei said. "He's used to inhaling his food. As long as he doesn't choke, he should be good to go." He winked at her.

Victoria simply shook her head. While Erik was the fastest eater, she was the slowest one. Between bites she nursed her ginger ale to calm her stomach. She was able to keep it all down.

She found it odd how comfortable eating with the family was. She wasn't even as relaxed with her own family. No one asked how long they knew each other, which Victoria was grateful for. They seemed to welcome and appreciate her just the same.

"Anybody care for some dessert?" Mrs. Rusak

asked after they'd nearly finished all the food in front of them. "We have sweet potato pie, chocolate cake, and lemon pudding. Take your pick, or in Erik's case, just decide on which one you want to try first."

They all laughed and Erik grinned back.

Since it was nice out, they went down on the patio to have their dessert and coffee. Victoria was able to see the lake better out there. As night started to fall, the lake sparkled with the setting sun, giving off an orange sparkle that spread across the water.

"A baby?" Andrei's father asked. "Are sure you're ready for a third kid?"

"Andrei Rusak Senior, if you don't leave your boy alone, I am going to get upset." Mrs. Rusak stared him. "Do you want me upset?"

"No but—"

"All right then. Either congratulate our son or keep your upsetting opinions in your law firm where they belong."

Although the man seemed agitated and seemed

unhappy about being quieted by his wife, he didn't say another word to them.

Erik leaned over. "Andrei said that I can be Uncle Erik. You don't mind that, do you, Victoria?"

"Of course not. That sounds fitting since Andrei sees you as family," Victoria said.

That put a big smile on Erik's face. "So Victoria, do you have any single friends looking for a good guy? Erik asked.

"Erik," Andrei warned.

"What? Can't blame a guy for asking."

"I have a few friends."

"Well, you name the time and place and I will be there," he said.

"I'll keep that in mind." His grin seemed to be a mile long.

"How did you and Andrei meet?" Amy asked.

Victoria liked Andrei's sister, who also looked more like Mr. Rusak than Mrs. Rusak, making Andrei taking on more of her features.

"We met in Judge Hughes's courtroom," Victoria said. "I am an Assistant Prosecuting Attorney for New York City. Your brother was defending the accused against me."

"Ooh," Amy said. "Which one of you won?"

"We can't talk about ongoing cases," Mr. Rusak said.

"Where are you from?" Mrs. Rusak added, ignoring her husband's comment.

"I moved here from California. As a matter of fact, my family still is out there," Victoria said. "I have been trying to get them to move to New York for the longest time, but they love the West Coast too much to leave."

That statement made her think about her choice to stay in the city or not. Although she didn't love New York, there were other reasons why she needed to stay.

"Don't worry," Mrs. Rusak said. "After you have the baby, you won't be able to keep them away. Parents love grandkids too much for that. When is the baby due?"

"The beginning of next year," Victoria said.

"Well, that gives me plenty of time to knit some winter suits for the little one. We don't want him or her getting a cold in the winter New York weather.

"That sounds lovely. Thank you."

"No problem at all. What do you want it to be? A boy or a girl?"

"Either one would be fine, as long as it is healthy. That's all that really matters to me."

"Yes, that's the main thing. Good health. So many new parents take that for granted these days. All those technological advancements to choose great genes for your child and pick your perfect baby consume so many of my patients. All they should care about is having a strong and healthy baby."

"I couldn't agree more," Victoria said. "Whatever it is, I know I can depend on Andrei to be there." As she said the words, she realized they were truer than anything else. She'd only spent a few hours with his family, but she knew that Andrei would be there for her and their baby no matter what.

CHAPTER 19

VICTORIA

"WE'RE THROWING YOU A BABY SHOWER!" Deedee said as soon as Victoria returned to work the following Monday after staying with Andrei's family. Deedee and Rosalyn sat in her office as she walked in.

"She means she's throwing one," Rosalyn said. Her pout was obvious. "I'm just learning about this."

She shut her office door quickly. "Shut up! I can count on one hand the people who know I'm pregnant. I don't want anyone else to find out yet."

Deedee fanned her away. "Nonsense. You act like you being pregnant is some kind of bad curse or something. You should be ecstatic to bring a new life into the world."

"Give the girl a break, Deedee," Rosalyn said. "It's not like she's been family planning or anything. This baby came out of nowhere. I'm sure they'd be all 'Yay, baby life' if they could."

"I'm still throwing you a baby shower, and you can't stop me. We have months to work out the details, but I'm getting this sucker ready."

Victoria wasn't ready to think about that far ahead just yet, so she switched topics by telling the girls about her weekend at Andrei's family's house. She described all the family members.

"Why in the hell are you still thinking about going to Chicago? That man is fine, girl, and his family sounds like they accept you. You need to know when to accept a good thing when it shows up like that."

"Forget the family. He said he loved you?"

"Yeah. He did."

"Do you love him?"

That was the question she'd been trying to answer over and over again without any final decision. It had been so hard to even consider loving someone so quickly, but it took going to his family's place and meeting them to know for certain.

"I do. I love him, which is why I'm talking to Smith this afternoon."

"And telling him what?" Deedee asked.

"I'm not going to Chicago. I've decided to stay here."

"Thank God. I was hoping you weren't going to do something so stupid as leave. Thought I was going to have to knock some sense into you."

Victoria rubbed her belly. "You can try, but as a protective mother, I think I should warn you I'm not going down without a fight."

"Good," Deedee said.

Rosalyn nodded. "We wouldn't expect anything less."

Visiting Smith's office this time was nowhere near as intimidating as it was the first time she'd gone in there to discuss Andrei and the possible promotion.

Victoria knew what she wanted. The tall, blond, and sexy defense attorney had caught her attention the first time she saw him, but she never knew how important he'd become to her.

"Are you sure about this, Bellamy?" Smith asked. "Once you turn this down, there's no guarantee something like this will come around again."

Victoria took a deep breath. "Can I be frankly honest with you, sir?" she asked.

He studied her for a bit before replying. "Go ahead."

"I probably seem like a complete idiot for not taking this position, and if this were a few months ago, I would have jumped on it. The last time we spoke, you told me that no matter how much I wanted to make a difference in this kind of work, I would never be able to put in the type of dedication as a person with a family. If I'm being truthful, I think you're right. But the problem was that I saw that as a bad thing."

Victoria took a deep breath and steadied herself as she explained her reasoning.

"Go on," Smith encouraged. "I'm listening."

"The reason I took this job isn't as big and

complicated as saving the world. That's great that people want to do that, but I'm a realist. The truth is that people can make a difference, but they can't make big changes overnight. If there is one thing this job has taught me, it's that bad people will always be out there hurting others and messing with good people."

"Although I could do some great work as the DA in Chicago, I know I've made a difference right here in this city. I know turning it down may disappoint you, but the truth is if I leave here, I'll disappoint myself. If I do that, it doesn't matter whether I'm the DA or just another ADA. I can't help anyone and put the right people away who deserve it."

He stared at her, but she didn't break. She looked right back as if she were in a trial and proving her case. Even when the meanest bastard stared back at her, she didn't waver because she knew justice would prevail when she did everything in her power to try a case fairly and accurately.

Even though she felt like she was the one on trial, she held her ground just the same and waited. If he thought she should be let go, that was his decision to make. Whatever happened, she didn't regret her decision.

"I knew I hired you for a reason," he said.

What he said threw her off. "Excuse me, sir?"

"Everyone around here knows I'm a hard ass, but it isn't because I want to fuck with people. It's because that's the only way I can tell who has the salt to make it in this office. We see so much awful shit every day that those who can't deal with me won't be able to do this job for long. I'm nothing when it comes to the mess we see done out there. I recommended you for the position because I know you can do some great things. Now, you've proved that you can speak your mind to me without worrying if I'll like what you say or not. I still don't approve of your choice, but I can respect that, and Bellamy, once a colleague earns my respect, it's something that never goes away."

"Thank you, sir."

"Now get back to work, Bellamy. If you're staying here, you might as well do some of that good you were talking about."

She nodded. "Yes, sir." She got up to leave, not sure whether she felt pride in her achievement, appreciation for not getting fired, or both.

"And Victoria?"

She turned back, a little stunned that he'd used her first name.

"I think you've earned the right to call me Andrew, but not in front of the interns. Don't want them getting big-ass heads around here."

"Yes, sir. I mean Andrew. Thank you."

He nodded and went back to his work.

As soon as she got back to her desk, she could hear her ringtone. When Victoria saw Andrei calling her phone, her smile was hard to hide, and she had no intention of doing so.

"Hey, beautiful," Andrei said.

"Hi," she said.

"You sound happy."

"I am very happy."

"Well, let's keep the good streak going. Join me for dinner tonight."

"You're cooking again? If you keep this up, you're going to bruise my domestic ego."

"No. I thought it be nice to go out tonight. Somewhere nice and overly expensive."

"Overly expensive, huh?"

"Yeah. I hear some people like those places."

That sounded like the perfect time to tell him her good news. "That sounds amazing. I can't wait." It also could be the place to finally give him the words he wanted to hear from her. Even though she knew how much she cared about him, a tiny part of her worried. He could always change his mind like her ex. There would always be that possibility of him leaving, but maybe

"Great. I'm sending a special package coming to you. Look out for it."

She giggled. "What kind of package?"

"If I told you, it wouldn't be special. Do you mind

if I pick you up from work? Promise I'll wait outside this time."

It warmed her throughout that he respected her to ask. Maybe she did overthink things too much. Besides, Andrei was nothing like any of the men she dated. He was in a brand new category all to himself, and it was one that she could appreciate in the longrun.

"Yes, you may come pick me up. I'd actually love that."

"Good. I'll see you at five-thirty."

"I get off at five."

"You'll need time to use my gift."

She bit her lip, curious as to what he was sending her way. "You better not be sending me something risqué, or I swear you're going to get it when I get to your place."

"Is that a promise?"

She leaned back in her chair. "You're awful."

"You won't say that when you see my surprise. I

promise you'll like." She heard someone call for him on his side of the phone. "I have to get to court. Promise me you'll follow the directions."

"What directions."

"Just promise me."

She had no clue what the hell he was talking about, but she was in a good mood. "Fine. I promise."

"Good. I have to go. I love you." He hung up before she got the chance to say it back. Before it had thrown her off guard and shocked her. Now, she felt bad that he'd felt so strongly about her and she'd given him no reason to think she even was thinking the same way.

It had taken her a bit to get over how quickly their relationship had happened. Sure, it wasn't like regular relationships, but what was a regular relationship? If she was honest with herself, she'd never been in one, so it shouldn't be odd for her to have another one.

She had lunch in her office with Rosalyn and Deedee, who were excited she decided to stay and curious at what Andrei was sending.

"I bet he's sending you roses," Deedee said.

Victoria thought back to when he brought her. "He's already pulled that move. This seems different for some reason."

A knock on the door interrupted them.

A delivery man stood in the doorway carrying a large box. "Delivery for Victoria Bellamy?" he said.

"That's me." Victoria went over and took the electronic board he handed her.

"Sign here please."

She had to focus on signing her name, since she kept glancing over at the box in his hand. "Thank you," she said when he handed it to her.

"What is it?" Deedee asked as she took it to her desk.

"I have no idea."

Deedee ran her hands over the closed box. "It's definitely not flowers."

Rosalyn chuckled. "You think?" She shook her

head. "Well, open it before we tear it open for you."

"Oh no. No one will be tearing anything." She gently opened the box and found a note inside: *Wear this for me tonight. I know it will look delicious on you. Love, Andrei.*

She folded the note so she could keep it for herself. Her friends didn't need that bit of information. Instead, she pulled out the covered item for them to see.

"Lover boy sent you that?" Rosalyn asked.

"Well, damn," Deedee said.

The item he'd had sent was a dress that felt like butter in her hands. It was slightly gold but as she turned it over it seem to take on different colors as the sun shined through her office windows.

Although she had a few fancy evening dresses for nights out, the last thing she ever had money for was something as expensive as what she held.

"Your man has taste," Rosalyn said. "That's for sure."

Victoria laughed as she held the dress in front of her. "I can't argue with that."

"Hell, good thing you stayed," Deedee said. "Otherwise, someone who gets that for his woman wouldn't be single long." Deedee leaned over the box. "Something else is in there." She pulled out a smaller box that was underneath the tissue paper and lifted up a heel that matched the dress.

"He got you shoes, too?" Rosalyn asked.

Deedee scoffed. "Girl, these aren't just shoes." She ran her hand over the shoe. "This is fine, Italian leather at its best."

"How would you and your empty bank account know anything about Italian leather?"

"My paycheck doesn't know anything about two-thousand dollar shoes, but my Pinterest account loves some Italian leather and French silk. That's my porn these days."

"Two thousand dollars?" Rosalyn grabbed the other shoe and analyzed it. "I'm clearly dating the wrong men in this city."

"Does Mr. Lawyer have any friends?" Deedee

asked.

Victoria laughed and took her shoes out of her friends hands. "Maybe, but I have to get to work so I can finish early. Otherwise, I won't be enjoying any of this."

Her friends left eyes her gifts. Usually, something this extravagant would make her uncomfortable, but Andrei had told her she didn't know how to be taken care of. She ran her hands over the material. Accepting this felt like a good start.

When Victoria finally left her building, most of the other employees were gone. Only Rosalyn was left along with a few others. She felt a little awkward wearing such an expensive outfit. If the shoes were worth two thousand dollars, she didn't want to think about the value of the dress. That didn't mean she didn't feel beautiful after putting everything on, and she didn't want to disappoint Andrei. She'd done enough of that already.

Rosalyn whistled, and Victoria had never heard the woman whistle.

"You look amazing." Rosalyn said. "Like a princess or something."

"Thank you," Victoria said. She ran her hand down the front of her dress. It made her brown skin seem ethereal as the golden material sparkled. "I feel all giddy, and I'm never giddy."

"Good," Rosalyn said. "You deserve to have a good time out tonight."

"Thanks."

"Say hi to your boyfriend for us."

She so had to get used to that term, but it was growing on her. "I will."

CHAPTER 20

VICTORIA

VICTORIA FOUND Andrei waiting by a black luxury sedan along with a driver in full professional attire. It was Andrei who had all her attention. Although she'd seen him in suits before, the one he wore blew the others away.

He stood there in a dark brown, three-piece suit made of the finest material that matched her dress' coloring perfectly. The blond locks that she was so used to were slicked back well with a small strand dangling over his eye.

As she got closer, his cologne invaded her senses, and she savored the exotic and musky smell of him. The people who passed them couldn't take their eyes off him.

Andrei walked over to her, gave her a hug, and kissed her on the cheek. "I knew you'd look gorgeous in that dress." He leaned in closer and whispered in her ear. "I can't wait to take it off you later."

He was in a very good mood, and she realized she liked that playful side of him. That was something she never did much. Her job made her serious twenty-four seven.

"Are you ready for tonight?" he asked.

"Depends on what you have in mind." She ran her hand over the front of his suit, enjoying the feel of it on him.

"Dinner awaits." He waived the driver off and opened the door for her.

"Good, because I'm starving," she winked at him before getting in, which was a little bit of a task.

"Careful or we won't make it to the restaurant." He shut her door once she was in the car and went to the other side to get in next to her.

"I would have gotten a limousine, but I thought

that was too reminiscent of prom days, and I didn't want to do that."

"Good call."

"I thought so." He pulled her over into his arms, and she settled there comfortably.

The driver pulled off without being asked, and Victoria enjoyed the silence. Traffic would have been a nightmare if she had been driving, and she wasn't even sure she could handle Andrei driving in rush hour traffic. The driver moved fluidly between the cars, letting all stress of the other cars and horns float by her so she was in her own little bubble with Andrei.

It took about a half an hour to get to their destination in traffic, although the place didn't seem too far away. She realized they were close to Andrei's place.

The sign above the restaurant entrance read "The Jewel Room." It was a place Victoria hadn't been to before, but by the fancy entrance with two stone lions and a fancy awning with matching red carpet, she knew it was an expensive place to eat.

She looked at the entrance, curious but still feeling out of her element. "Are you sure were at the right place?"

"I wanted to bring you somewhere special," Andre said.

"My parents love this place. They know the owner, so he did me a favor."

"What kind of a favor?"

"You'll just have to wait and see."

"You've had me waiting a lot today."

"Come on. You know the saying. All good things come to those who wait, and I promise some good things are definitely coming." He opened her door and held out his hand for her.

"I'm going to hold you to that."

"I wouldn't expect anything less."

The inside of the restaurant was fabulous and breathtaking. Chandeliers with candles filled the ceilings, while lit candelabras lined the walls. It felt like shit step back into a different period of time as Andrei led her inside.

She held onto his arm tight, afraid if she didn't should wake up from some kind of weird fantasy sequence. "This place is amazing."

"I knew you'd like it."

The city was busy outside of the restaurant, so it was odd not to see anyone else but workers inside.

"Where is everyone?"

"Like I said, I had the owner give me a favor. The whole restaurant is ours tonight."

"You rented out an entire restaurant for me?"

"You're my woman," Andrei said with a sly smile. "You're worth it."

Only one table stood in the middle of the expansive dining room area, and it had white flowers on the table as a center piece. Two chairs sat at the table next to each other along with a matching set of dinnerware.

Further back in the restaurant, a small waterfall rushed into a wishing well and soft classical music played in the background.

"This is a lot to take in, Andrei. I'm not used to this at all."

"We're not going to dine like this every night. Don't worry, but I did want to do something special for you, to show you how much I care about you. It's fit for a queen. My queen."

Victoria could feel her cheeks heat up at his words. If she was blushing this early in their evening, she didn't want to know what she'd feel like later on.

A waiter, dressed in a tuxedo, came over to them with a menu.

"Mr. Rusak, would you like some wine?" the man asked.

"Actually, we'll both be skipping the alcohol tonight. Bring us out some sparkling strawberry and kiwi juice."

The man bowed. "Right away, sir. Would you like to order now?"

"We'll have two of your Kobe steaks smothered in onions, mushrooms, and gravy along with two large cabbage leaves stuffed with wild rice and vegetables. For dessert, bring us the crème brulee bread pudding. Is that ok for you, honey?"

Victoria was surprised that he called her honey but most of all, she was shocked at how easily he had ordered for both of them without looking at the menu. "Yes. Sounds great." After the waiter left, she leaned into Andrei. "What are we celebrating?"

"Who says we have to be celebrating something? Can't a guy just take his girl out for a good time?"

"I guess that depends on the guy and the girl he's taking out."

"In that case, it's just you and me tonight, baby."

He was really getting used to using endearments when it came to her, and it made her wonder what she should call him in return.

"Okay, sugar lips," she said.

"Sugar lips? Where did that come from?"

"You're such a smooth talker that I thought it would work. I'm going to have to get back to you on that one."

"Good thinking, because I'm not sure I could face my siblings ever again if you called me about in front of them. They'd never let me live it down."

The waiter brought out their drinks.

"I think we should make a toast," Andrei said, lifting up his glass.

Victoria eyed him suspiciously, but she still lifted up her glass along with him. "Okay. What should we toast to?"

"To the happiest day of my life. I have finally met the woman who I want to spend the rest of my life with. A woman who is so intelligent, considerate, and passionate that she makes me want to spend every day and night with her."

Victoria couldn't move as she watched Andrei get down on one knee. "Victoria Bellamy, my life is so empty without you. I didn't know how much until I met you. I know we don't have the most conventional relationship known to man, but that doesn't mean we don't have something that can make us happy for the rest of our lives. Will you make me whole and do me one of the greatest honors possible by marrying me?"

Victoria took everything in. All of it. The staff members watching them in the distance, the beautiful surroundings that gave background to that romantic moment, and most of all the amazing man who had stolen her heart without her even knowing it.

She didn't cry. She was usually a crier, but the baby and Andrei's family had brought out emotions in her that she had long since forgotten. Tears welled in her eyes even though she had to get used to how sappy they were making her. She finally found her voice so she could respond. "Yes, Andrei Rusak. I will marry you?"

A wave of relief filled Andrei's face as he placed the beautiful emerald-cut, three-carat diamond on her ring finger.

Victoria was still in shock as tears ran down her face. For the longest time, she doubted that he could have actual feelings for her. His proposal only confirmed what his actions in the words had done leading up to it.

Andrei pulled her up into his arms, and she

realized there was no better place she'd rather be than right there with him.

When he finally kissed her, she felt her usual sensations of longing and desire. But deeper than that, she felt wanted and needed.

"I love you. Now and always, Victoria."

"I love you, too," she said. When the smile grew on his face, she repeated the other words. "Now and always."

EPILOGUE

ANDREI

"THIS CASE IS RIDICULOUS, ANDREI." Victoria sat up in bed with a stack of papers all around her. "You can't really believe he's innocent."

Andrei ran a nice, hot bath for her and returned to the bedroom to find her still reading legal documents. He couldn't believe that their baby would be coming in one month. His very pregnant fiancé looked beautiful, even though the woman didn't know when to take a break to save her life.

He was at least grateful that her job had given her early maternity leave so she could rest, and although he had gotten her to promise not to do any of her work while she was off, he realized he hadn't said anything about his cases. Leave it to a lawyer to find their way out of a verbal commitment.

"I know, baby," he said. "That's why I'm leaving those cases for my father and Sam to defend. I told you, I'm not doing criminal cases anymore. It's medical malpractice all the way, especially since my father's letting me open up a new office to focus on that."

"I still can't believe you got him to accept your proposition."

"With you on my team, was there any doubt?"

"I can argue pretty damn well, can't I?" she asked.

"Let's put it this way. I will never go up against you in the courtroom ever again."

"Are you giving up fighting against me already, love?"

He enjoyed the endearment for him she had settled on, especially since it meant she said his favorite word to him every time she used it.

Andrei crawled into bed next to her and kissed her beautiful belly with their baby resting peacefully inside before kissing her. "I've come to see that fighting with you is so much better than fighting against."

"Oh, really?" She watched him above the papers in her hand.

"Absolutely."

The fireplace was lit to warm up the bedroom, and he'd gotten some hot chocolate for them to enjoy. Even now, he wanted her as much as ever with her addictive skin glowing and those growing breasts tempting him. He'd tried to ease up fulfilling his constant need for her, but Victoria would have none of it. In fact, it seemed like her libido increased with every trimester.

"You were supposed to be reading about possible wedding venues, remember?" he teased. He moved all the papers, so she couldn't read them anymore.

"But planning a wedding is so stressful. Law is so much more interesting."

"If you keep avoiding it, I'm going to think you don't want to marry me."

Her eyes widened. "Never. I am meeting you at the end of that aisle, Rusak. You can count on that."

"Glad to hear it," Andrei said. "Now are you going to join me for that bath, or do I have to bathe alone, and I really hate bathing alone." He kissed her longer this time, so she'd feel how much he wanted her.

"Help me get out of my gown?"

"You don't have to ask me twice," said Andrei. He didn't wait for her to go to their bathroom. He lifted her up into his arms and carried her there himself.

"I'm not an invalid, Andrei."

"Shut up and let me carry my soon-to-be wife to our bath."

"Fine. Just so you know I could have walked here perfectly well on my own."

He chuckled. "I would never assume such a ridiculous thing."

They had a huge garden tub in their new condo, large enough for four people to fit comfortably, so they both had plenty of room when they had downtime like this.

He helped Victoria out of her gown and eased her into the warm water, and then he disrobed and climbed in behind her. He loved how soft she felt naked against him, right where she belonged.

He poured some of her favorite floral bath soap in a sponge and worked on her back and shoulders. She moaned and wiggled against him and he felt his cock reacting to her luscious movements.

"You little minx, keep that up, and I can't guarantee I won't take that squirming body of yours."

"Promises, promises," she taunted.

He wasn't going to let her get away with that. All pretenses of washing her back flew out the window, and he turned her chin up until he could capture her soft mouth with his. She always tasted so good and ready for him. He loved that she would be his not long after their little boy arrived.

Andrei was used to winning in his professional life, but when he found Victoria, he far outdid anything he could have achieved on his own. He couldn't wait to spend the rest of his life with both of them and his two girls. He had a complete family now, and that was better than any case he could have ever won.

EPILOGUE II

VICTORIA

"ANDREI, have you seen my lip gloss? My whole drawer is empty?"

"No, babe." Andrei came in from the bathroom with a towel wrapped around his waist, looking good enough to eat. "I don't really pay attention to your lip gloss."

"I have fifty gazillion things of flavored lip gloss, but I have no idea where all of it is." I showed Andrei the empty drawer. "Where on earth could it be?"

Just then, Benjamin walked into the room.

"What did you do to yourself?" Victoria screeched.

His cheeks were covered in various shades of pink and icy brown lip gloss.

"I'm a football player, Daddy! Look at me!" In his arms, he held the small football that his grandfather had given him for his birthday. He ran to his father and tried to tackle him. He was not successful, partially because he was about the height of his father's knee. His lack of success wasn't related to a lack of effort though. He strained against his father's leg, clearly trying to push him over.

Instead of obliging his son and falling over, Andrei scooped him up. "What have you done to your face?"

"I used Mommy's paint to paint my face just like them."

"It's not lip gloss," Andrei said, clearly trying not to laugh. "It's black grease."

"Ew," Victoria squeaked. "Lip gloss is bad enough." She walked over to Andrei and pulled their son into her arms. "I need to wash you off." She walked past Andrei and into the bathroom. She wet a towel and gently wiped the lip gloss off of

Benjamin's face. She kissed his damp but clean cheek when she was done.

"Next time you want to be a football player, skip the war paint, okay?"

Instead of agreeing, Benjamin simply wiggled out of his mother's arms, landed on the tile floor, and headed for the bathroom door.

Andrei must have taken advantage of their son staying still for 30 seconds to put on some pants. He was fully dressed when Victoria came out of the bathroom. Benjamin was already running at full speed past his father and towards the stairs.

"Benjamin!" Victoria shouted. "Stop!"

Andrei caught the back of Benjamin's shirt in the nick of time, because if he'd been a fraction of a second slower, their kid would've taken a tumble down the stairs.

"I've told you a million times that we need another baby gate up here," Victoria said, her heart still going crazy.

"I'll get it tomorrow." Andrei pulled Benjamin close and kissed the top of his head. Victoria put her arms around the two of them, smelling the sweet scent of her baby's head and the warm musk of her husband.

"I would do anything to keep you two safe," Andrei murmured before he kissed her cheek.

"I love you both," Victoria said, "even though you're going to go to time out for scaring Mommy like that, buddy."

"Noooo!" Benjamin wailed. He started crying. The terrible twos had barely started, but Benjamin tried to have a tantrum as often as he could. He tried to get out of his father's grip and throw himself on the ground so he could kick and scream.

But Andrei held onto his son, a little grimly and very firmly.

"Now, son, you did something bad, so you have to be punished for it."

Benjamin sobbed, "No," but he was quieter this time.

"Real men take responsibility for their actions. We all make mistakes, but a big boy has to admit when he's wrong. You stole your mother's lip gloss and got dirty. What do you say to your mother?"

"I'm sorry," Benjamin whispered.

"I forgive you," Victoria said, kissing his chubby little cheek. "But no running towards the stairs anymore, okay?"

"If I promise, no timeout?"

"A born lawyer," Andrei observed with a wry smile.

"Deal," Victoria said, sharing a secret smile with her husband.

THE END